"I don't like this plan."

"You've made that clear," Maddie said as she rubbed her hand over his chest. He doubted she realized she was touching him as they hid there, waiting. But he knew. When this was over...

He couldn't think of that now. Now he had to keep her safe. The thought of her hurt—or worse—knocked the breath out of him.

He admired her spunk and determination. He couldn't imagine living half a life under the constant threat of death and the watchful eye of the government. Knowing that a criminal sat in a cell somewhere plotting against her made Adam want to issue a threat of his own.

His gaze went to her mouth, slipping down her long neck then back to those lips. He was going to kiss her. In the middle of a sting, with his men a short distance away. It had been building for days. Weeks. He'd dreamed about the smoothness of her skin and how it would feel to wrap her legs around his waist. Now he would live it.

He lowered his head and as he did, he heard the dreadful words in his earpiece. "He's coming."

HELENKAY DIMON

LOCKED AND LOADED

Harlequin®

TORONTO NEW YORK LONDON
AMSTERDAM PARIS SYDNEY HAMBURG
STOCKHOLM ATHENS TOKYO MILAN MADRID
PRAGUE WARSAW BUDAPEST AUCKLAND

Recycling programs
for this product may
not exist in your area.

ISBN-13: 978-0-373-74618-7

LOCKED AND LOADED

Copyright © 2011 by HelenKay Dimon

This edition published by arrangement with Harlequin Books S.A.

For questions and comments about the quality of this book please contact
us at Customer_eCare@Harlequin.ca.

www.Harlequin.com

Printed in U.S.A.

ABOUT THE AUTHOR

Award-winning author HelenKay Dimon spent twelve years in the most unromantic career ever—divorce lawyer. After dedicating all that effort to helping people terminate relationships, she is thrilled to deal in happy endings and write romance novels for a living. Now her days are filled with gardening, writing, reading and spending time with her family in and around San Diego. HelenKay loves hearing from readers, so stop by her website at www.helenkaydimon.com and say hello.

Books by HelenKay Dimon

HARLEQUIN INTRIGUE

1196—UNDER THE GUN*
1214—NIGHT MOVES
1254—GUNS AND THE GIRL NEXT DOOR*
1260—GUNNING FOR TROUBLE*
1297—LOCKED AND LOADED*

*Mystery Men

CAST OF CHARACTERS

Adam Wright—This Recovery Project agent is stuck miles from home, babysitting a woman who is desperate to ignore him. He spends his days hovering over a computer and watching Maddie from afar...and his nights figuring out how to get a lot closer.

Maddie Timmons—She is a tough woman in an impossible spot. She paid for a bad relationship in the past with a broken back, a criminal investigation and a new identity thanks to the Witness Security Program. Now she needs help and that handsome computer hottie next door might be the answer.

Trevor Walters—A guarded, powerful and respected businessman. He's made an informal agreement with the Recovery Project that might protect him, but he has other secrets...ones that could get them all killed.

Rod Lehman—The man who assembled the Recovery Project team. His off-the-books investigation into missing women in the Witness Security Program puts all the Recovery agents in danger.

John Tate—As the government administrator who decides who gets into witness protection he wields a tremendous amount of power. What he uses it for is the question.

Vince Ritter—He stays on the fringes of the Recovery Project, providing information and offering help. The problem is telling which side he's actually on.

Luke Hathaway—The interim head of the Recovery Project. He has the unenviable job of making everything work. When he adds "keeping Maddie alive" to his list of tasks, he fears he's made Adam and the entire team targets.

Chapter One

Maddie Timmons turned over in bed for what felt like the fiftieth time. It had to be past two by now, but she refused to look at the clock and check. Not again.

The room had plunged into darkness hours ago when the sun ducked behind the mountains outlining the side of her cabin. The cool late-spring air couldn't penetrate the thick windows near her head. She knew because she'd installed the laminated safety glass herself and then made sure the potential entrances stayed locked at all times. A security alarm took care of the rest.

She kicked off the covers and stared at the ceiling. Despite all the precautions, something made her restless. She couldn't pinpoint a reason. She just knew her insides kept jumping around, pressing down on her chest and

forcing her eyes open every time they tried
to drift shut.

The unease had crept up on her that afternoon while she'd worked the lunch rush at the
diner, doing the baking and serving the meals.
Though in Sweet Home, West Virginia, the
weekday "rush" usually meant about thirty
people over the span of three hours.

She sat up and felt the mattress dip beneath
her. Just as her feet hit the hardwood floor, the
banging started on her front door. She heard
the thud and the faint sound of a male voice
calling her name.

The late hour. The frantic attempt to wake
her. It all struck her as wrong.

Every nerve ending in her body screamed
for her to run. Her cottage was blocked from
the neighbor's by towering trees, and the dark
night would give her attackers the advantage.
And she could not risk getting caught. Ever.

She slid her feet into the white sneakers
that always sat by her bed. The knife she kept
under her pillow slipped neatly into the waistband of her pajama shorts. She had to grab her
bag and take off.

That was the plan. Get to safety and then
call the number she'd memorized for a situa-

tion just like this. The same emergency she'd hoped would never arrive.

She crept across the floor and wrapped her fingers around the handle of her packed safety bag. She listened closely for any sounds of house penetration. Relief flowed through her when only quiet echoed back.

She rounded the corner and headed for the small secret opening to the space under the house. From there she could see the property and listen for footsteps. Then it was just a practiced run to safety.

"Maddie?"

She froze. The husky whisper sounded louder and deeper than before. And totally familiar.

She eased the duffel back to the floor in total silence. The mandatory escape plan ran through her mind, but she ignored it. Instead, she walked down the short hall that led to the family room. The cabin consisted of exactly two rooms plus a kitchen and bath. No matter how careful she was, how shadowed the rooms, she would come into view from one of the windows in two more steps.

"Maddie?" The knocking grew louder and showed no signs of stopping.

Her brain pleaded for caution. Every other part of her wanted to open the door.

With quiet steps, she crossed the smooth floor and flattened her stomach against the front door. A quick look through the peephole confirmed what she already knew. Adam Wallace wanted in.

She hesitated, thinking of all the ways this could be a trap, but reached for the locks anyway. Metal rattled in her shaking fingers as she rushed to get the door open.

He stood there, all six foot three of him. Sandy-blond hair, thin wire glasses and shoulders wider than the door frame. He was her next-door neighbor. The chatty, sexy computer nerd with the linebacker body who moved in and insisted they be friends, all while she dodged every attempt.

She grabbed the side of the door and carefully blocked his way into the house, knowing he could power through if he really wanted to.

"What's wrong?" she asked.

"That's my question."

She had never seen him do this frantic-whisper thing. Sure, they'd only known each other a month, but he'd been so even-keeled all that time. "Adam, I don't—"

He pushed the frames up on his nose. "I heard a noise."

The implication of that statement hit her full force. Blood pounded in her ears. "What? Where?"

"I was watching a movie and thought I heard something crash over here. I came to make sure you were okay."

As quickly as the adrenaline flooded her senses it receded again. No need to panic—yet. This likely was about a guy being lonely and nothing more. Why someone his age would choose to live out here, all alone, was a constant mystery. That question made her wary of him, just as she was wary of everyone else. She had to be.

But she did wonder how a man who towered over her and possessed those impressive arm muscles could look so sweet and comfortably disheveled at all times. Probably had something to do with the dimple in his cheek.

But he wasn't smiling now. Energy thrummed off him as he glanced all around, barely looking at her.

"So, are you okay?" he asked.

"Of course."

He finally focused his attention on her. The power of those grass-green eyes almost

knocked her flat. Intelligence lingered there…
and something else. Something she couldn't
pin down. His size signaled danger but his
easygoing manner made her think geek. The
guy was an enigma.

"Can I come in?" he asked.

"No." The answer was automatic. Forget
her curiosity and the hint of attraction. The
response was the right one.

"Excuse me?"

Her grip tightened on the door. "It's late."

The frenzied moments faded as his eyebrow
inched up. "I came over to make sure nothing
had happened to you."

"And I'm fine, so we're good." She couldn't
let him in—physically or emotionally. If he'd
truly heard something, if danger lingered
in the woods surrounding her unwanted
adopted home, then she had to run. Dragging
a computer nerd with her would only slow her
down. And the rules were clear: travel alone
and light.

"Okay." He wiped a hand through his thick
hair. With one last look behind him, he leaned
in, sending warm air across her cheek. "If you
need me, yell."

"I'm—"

"Fine. Yeah, I know. You said that already.

Many times." He blew out a long breath. "Just promise me."

Gone was the harmless cutie who'd caught her eye and kept it by coming into the diner every afternoon while she was on duty. He ordered pie and coffee and tipped her twice the bill. He never varied the scene…or he hadn't until today. He'd always smiled and laughed, flirted and then left with a "well, I tried" mumble when she made it clear those efforts were going to waste.

That was then. Now his jaw clenched and his mouth flattened. The dimple disappeared the second she turned him down.

"Maddie?"

"I promise I'll scream if I need you." It was a little lie, so she didn't feel any guilt in telling it.

"Okay." He shifted but didn't leave. "I'll be close by."

Sounded like a threat to her, so she shut the door in his face before he could say anything else. The locks clicked under her fingers as she studied him through the peephole and saw he continued to stand on her front porch.

He paced around as if fighting some internal battle. It took another few minutes for him to jog down the steps and head for his house.

The thudding of her heart took longer to slow. For the first time since he introduced himself, he scared her. Sent her mind racing in a hundred different directions at once. And this wasn't the first time today. He'd lingered at the diner this afternoon, being more flirty than usual. He'd acted as if…

A smile spread across her lips before she could fight it off. Now that she ran down the clues it all made sense. This wasn't about noises or concerns for her safety. The man was looking for a temporary bed partner.

She had to take responsibility for that. She'd given in and sat down in the booth with him for a few minutes today. For once, she'd returned the harmless flirting. That sweet smile of his had done it. His mouth had kicked up and she'd turned to mush. She'd always preferred bad boys—and look where that got her. Giving a hunky nerd some attention had felt right for a change.

Adam was more than two hundred pounds of sweet temptation, but the seduction stuff had to end. She couldn't afford ties and refused to trust anyone who just popped into her life out of thin air. Starting tomorrow, she'd build the wall back up between them and hit him with a flashing stop sign until he turned his attention somewhere else.

She felt a kick in her gut at the thought of him finding someone else to joke with, and the feeling had nothing to do with fear. It was more like regret. The same emotion she'd lived with her entire adult life. But she'd survived it before and she would figure out a way to handle it this time, too.

ADAM WRIGHT BRACED his back against the side of Maddie's house and listened. It was about three-thirty in the morning and he'd been waiting under her window for more than an hour. He'd tried to get into the room the logical way—through the front door and with an invitation—but Maddie was having none of it. Not that Maddie was her real name. Of course, Wallace wasn't his, either.

The Recovery Project, the now-private investigation firm he worked for, had been tracking her for months. They found missing people and Maddie was more than missing. She was supposed to be dead. If he didn't work fast, she would be.

According to their intel, the attackers would come tonight. Adam had seen the men roll into town earlier that evening, obviously out of place in their suits and black sedan. Fitting in around this part of West Virginia required a dependable pickup and jeans. Adam knew because he had been working the fake identity for more than a month. He'd abandoned the contacts in favor of glasses, temporarily traded his condo in D.C. for a one-bedroom cabin in the middle of nowhere.

People in town knew him as the guy who did computer work. In reality, he was a deep undercover. A former government agent on a mission to find his missing boss and figure out what role Maddie played in the corruption within the Witness Security Program, WitSec. For now he would treat her as a potential victim and then make sure the "potential" never turned into a reality.

At a crouch, he walked around the back of the house and along the opposite side. The sensor lights she'd installed didn't click on because he'd disabled them. He'd spent a day wandering around in the dark, figuring out how to trigger her alarm and then another day learning how to get around it.

He used that knowledge now. He slipped a small metal box out of his pocket and held it to the wall next to the back door. The handheld computer lit up as it wirelessly hooked into her alarm and turned it off. The plastic key in his front pocket got him the rest of the way into her house.

The place was small and deadly dark. Not even the air moved. For a second he worried he'd waited too long, that she was already gone, but that wasn't possible. He'd been watching, just hoping someone would make a move on her so he could react.

The boredom of behind-the-desk surveillance was killing him slowly. A man could only eat so much diner pie before his gut messed up his shot. He enjoyed that part of his cover, but he couldn't afford to get soft. Or stupid.

But the days of lying around, watching out his window and checking in with his fellow Recovery Project agents long-distance were over. No more waiting. He was going to grab her and get her out of there.

Since all the cabins had been built long ago as temporary residences for forest service employees, the layout of this one mirrored his own. In a few steps he stopped at her bedroom door. When he didn't hear screaming or anything else, he turned the knob.

Without any sound, he stepped across the

threshold, his eyes focusing on the rumpled bed. The empty bed.

Yelling and aiming a lamp for his skull, she launched her attack. She flew at him from the left side. She was all over him, scratching and kicking, screaming threats and promises of pain. She jumped on his back as her fists pounded against his shoulders.

The base of the lamp glanced off his upper back. The spot went numb, but he couldn't take a second to check it. He doubled over to throw her off balance. As her feet left the floor, his hands caught hers. He tried to fend off the blows without hurting her. He would if he had to. Hell, he'd knock her out if it came to that. He just hoped it didn't.

"Maddie, stop," he hissed at her.

"Get out!" Her hands smacked against the side of his head. She fought as though death was at her heels. "Now!"

He spun her around and grabbed her from behind, locking her arms to her sides. The trapped position didn't stop her thrashing. She shifted and wiggled and made it nearly impossible to hold her still.

Someone had taught her to fight dirty. If Adam weren't so busy getting knocked around, he might have admired her effort. But he didn't have time for that now.

He grumbled in her ear. "They'll hear you."

The fighting ended as her body went still, as if the life was sucked right out of her. "What?"

"They're here."

Tension radiated off every muscle. "Who?"

"The two men making their way through the woods to get to you." He thought about easing up on his viselike grip but decided against it. This lady was no slacker. She would throw him through the window if she got the chance. "I have to get you out of here."

She looked over her shoulder, her sky-blue eyes wild. "You're a computer geek."

He ignored the slam since he'd heard it all the time. Hitting the gym every day didn't stop the perception. "You've been compromised. Your WitSec handler was dirty. He sold you out."

As fast as her anger rose, her face went blank. "I don't know what you're talking about."

Yeah, that was the party line. Denial. Adam got it, even understood the reason for the web of secrecy, but it worked against them right now. Pretending ignorance could get them killed.

"We don't have time for this." He lifted her off her feet and dragged her through the house toward the front door, which wasn't easy since she'd turned to dead weight in his arms.

"You can't—"

"Stop talking." At her openmouthed stare, he softened his tone. "If they didn't hear all that screaming, we might still have a chance to get away." Something in his words kicked up a second round of attack. As they walked, she put her feet out, balancing them on either side of the doorway and bringing them to a shuddering stop.

"Maddie, you have to—"

"Let me go." This time her voice stayed at the level of a harsh whisper.

He watched the green lights streak through the woods. "The men are here. We're out of time."

"I'm not going anywhere with you."

Holding both her hands in one of his, he pointed into the darkness and didn't let up until her gaze followed his direction. "See those lights? They're coming for you."

"You don't know that."

He ignored her denials. "Right now, in the middle of the woods. They found you and will not stop until they get you."

She shook her head, sending her deep auburn hair over her shoulders. "It can't be."

"This isn't a friendly visit. They are here to kill you." Adam didn't bother prettying up the details. He needed her to understand before they both ended up dead in shallow graves. "I'll explain it all, but later."

A tremor shook through her. "You did this."

"No." He regained his double-fisted hold before she wrenched an arm loose and started hitting him again. "I'm here to save you."

She stopped fidgeting. "How?"

"We run."

Chapter Two

He knew she was in witness protection. No one should know. No one *could* know, not if she wanted to live.

Maddie inhaled, trying to slow her frantic heartbeat and come up with a plan. She focused on her training, on all the drills she'd run since she'd landed in the tiny town and slipped under the chilly blanket of anonymity.

Every brain cell screamed at her to take Adam down and run as fast as she could and not stop until she cleared the West Virginia line. She could handle the racing part. The question was how to win a battle against a man who outweighed her by a good seventy pounds.

At five-eight with long legs and a runner's form, she rarely viewed her body as petite, but Adam loomed over her. Feeling small filled her with a twinge of vulnerability. She hated the sensation. It made her jumpy. Amazing how just when she thought she'd knocked all those useless emotions out of her brain, one came roaring back to crush her.

But she beat the insecurities back. Right now she needed all her control and concentration. "I know the way."

He didn't ease his grip on her arms. "Yeah, it's called a back door."

"Too obvious."

"I'm listening."

She ignored the tickle of his hot breath against her neck. "There's a secret exit."

"Show me."

When he didn't ask why she would have such a thing, or even flinch at the idea, she knew Adam Wallace—or whoever he really was—was not a simple computer programmer. His wrestling moves said mercenary. His knowledge of the most private part of her life made him downright dangerous.

So did being trapped in a small cabin with him. Attackers or not, she had to get outside. She'd get around them and then the next wave and anyone else who was tracking her down. That's what her life had become—one long run to nowhere.

Open space was her only chance. That meant

giving away the location of her escape hatch. Not that she'd need it now. With her cover blown, she'd be shuffled to a new state with a new identity. From there on she'd pull her life in tighter around her so as not to risk a night like tonight.

But she had to live through this mess first.

She tried to swivel around but couldn't move. "You have to let go of me."

"Not going to happen."

"If we're just going to stand here, you better figure out how close our visitors are. I'd hate to die because you're busy making a plan and not moving from the middle of a room."

"Fine." He let go of her but kept his hands right by her shoulders, as if ready to grab her again if needed. "Talk."

Matching his caution, she turned, barely letting her feet leave the floor. His hands found her forearms and only a foot of air separated them. At this distance she saw the sweet guy who tipped big after dessert had changed into someone lethal and commanding.

"It's in the hallway," she said.

"What is?"

"My escape route."

"Let's see it." He walked her back toward

the bedroom. His gaze bounced from her face to the windows beyond.

Even if she wanted to bolt, and she sure thought about it, she couldn't. The timing was wrong and the man was too big. He also seemed prepared for action and that gave her an odd sense of comfort in the surreal moment.

She pointed at the narrow closet. "There's an opening behind the ironing board. Though to look at you, I have no idea how you'll squeeze in there."

"I've never had a problem getting in before, no matter how tight the fit."

His sudden grin made her think they were talking about different things. "I bet."

"Where does it come out?"

"About twenty feet away, behind the small shed before the tree line."

"Open it." He glanced over her head. "And fast. We only have minutes before the doors and windows come blowing in."

She didn't bother lecturing him on chivalry or issuing orders. She didn't look behind her, either. A narrow green searchlight twice cut through the dark cabin while they stood there. She knew the men outside were getting close, had probably surrounded the house and cut off the obvious exits. Good thing she had a surprise one.

She threw open the door and with practiced efficiency removed the ironing board and fake panel behind it. The flashlight came next. She ripped it from the wall and tested it. "You ready?"

"I see *you* are."

"Always." She dropped to her knees and started crawling.

The dank air smacked her in the face as soon as she crossed the threshold. The heavy staleness stole her breath as fear raced through her mind. She couldn't think about what lived in her makeshift safety route or what would happen if they were caught before they could get out.

Her first handler, Rod Lehman, had insisted on her having an emergency exit no matter where she lived. The workmen who thought they were laying reinforcement pipe for the sewer helped, but she did all the work in the final connection to the cabin. Building and re-inforcing the tube in the dead silence of night had been quite an undertaking.

Once completed, she had set up an escape strategy and practiced shortening her time to the shed. One oversight was in conducting the drill in jeans. Now in her pajama shorts, the hard flooring hurt her knees and the coolness of the metal sent a chill through the rest of her.

And then there was the issue of creeping around with an unwanted partner. One who held her ankle and crowded against her the entire time.

"Could you move back and give me some room to move?" She shook her leg, trying to break his hold, but he didn't let go.

"Keep moving."

She did as he ordered. She sped up, trying to increase the space between their bodies and her chances of getting away. "Why should I trust you?"

"Because you don't have a choice."

Wrong. She'd let that be the excuse for the dead end her life had become. Well, no more.

She was done paying for her poor choices. Getting shipped from Chicago to Sweet Home, losing touch with everything and everyone she'd ever known, constituted a pretty big punishment in her mind. Her bad-boy, thrill-ride addiction was over. Likely so was her time in West Virginia.

She reached the end of the tube and grabbed for the handle of the door to pull her body up to a kneeling position. Spinning the dials, she put in the combinations and undid the series of locks. Silence filled the small area, but the tension pulsed hard enough to knock her over.

"Got it?" He reached around her and helped shove away the panel.

The tight space turned claustrophobic. His chest pressed against her back. His arms wrapped around her from each side, trapping her tight to his body. From his breath against her hair, to his knees wedging her feet against the outside walls of the space, she was surrounded. Imprisoned and unable to launch her desperate plan.

Fingers fumbling, she helped Adam unseal the last of the opening. The black night and cool reviving air greeted them. A ceiling of stars peeked through the thick walls of trees. She heard chirping and the rustle of branches in the wind.

"Looks clear." The words were almost soundless by her ear. "Climb out nice and slow until we're sure."

Her brain started a countdown. It ended when Adam grabbed a fistful of her shirt and held her in place.

"Don't even think about running." He guided her out and jumped to his feet before she could gain her balance. "I'm your best shot at staying alive."

If he was trying to make her feel better, he missed the mark by a good two miles. "They have the guns."

"They're not alone." He slipped one hand under her elbow and kept the other on the weapon that appeared in his hand as if by some demented magic trick.

"I thought you were one of the good guys."

"Why do you think I'm not?"

"The gun."

"You want a rescuer with a weapon. Trust me."

She didn't want a rescuer at all. "I'd prefer to get out of here."

"That's next." Adam pressed her back against the shed and slid his body against hers.

Pinned to a wall with his hard chest at her front, she couldn't move. His stance wasn't sexual or even overbearing. It was more protective than anything.

For the first time since he walked into the diner, he struck her as a man accustomed to giving orders and having them followed. The type of guy who rushed in to help when others ran away to safety. The exact opposite of a shy computer nerd.

The gun passed in front of her face for a second then was gone. He had one of her hands in his and her other was trapped against his broad chest. He wasn't looking at her, but she couldn't help looking at him. She wondered how she'd ever viewed him as harmless. Seeing him in action now, gun up and attitude firmly in place, she could smell the power on him. It mixed with the cool mint scent of his breath.

She swallowed, trying to block out everything but the slamming of her heart and the plan forming in her head. "Well?"

He shook his head. "I don't see them."

"What does that mean?"

"They could have breached the inside." He stepped back and brought her with him. They walked around the side of the shed until her cabin sat to their left and his stood at a fifty-yard dead run in front of them. "We're not going to wait to find out. We have to circle around my cabin and get to my car."

"Why not use mine?"

"They'd probably recognize it. Might have tampered with it."

His points made sense. Very logical, just a bit too informed for the man he was supposed to be.

But standing there was the wrong call, in her view. "Let's run while we can."

She had shifted only enough to get an unobstructed view of her house, when the snapping of a twig registered in her brain. A green light sliced across her yard to land on her stomach. Shock stopped her steps.

"Get down!"

Adam's voice barely registered. She saw his eyes widen and his mouth open on a shout. Everything else moved in slow motion. A figured appeared in front of her, clad all in black and aiming a weapon right at her head. She tried to see his face, but a helmet and mask covered him.

Her brain clicked to life just as a huge weight knocked into her from behind. Her knees buckled and the ground inched closer. Arms wrapped around her chest, banding and confining her, half cushioning her fall and half pushing her deeper into the dirt.

The thud and bounce against the hard earth pushed a grunt up her throat as her bones rattled. Every muscle screamed in agony from the force of the fall.

Her legs wrapped around something and kept her locked in a deadman's position. The shove could have taken five seconds or five days. She couldn't tell. Time slowed until the whoosh of the air around her became a moaning call.

That fast the weight lifted. One minute she saw the attacker stalking toward her, the next her face pressed into Adam's back. Flat on her stomach with leaves scratching her cheek, she found her body shielded by Adam as soft pings echoed around her. His body kicked back against her as he fired his weapon.

She lifted her head in time to see the commando at her back door drop to his knees then fall face-first down the short steps. He hit the bush she'd always hated and meant to remove. Another man lay off to her right, facedown. She hadn't even seen that one coming.

Then the world stopped tilting. She dared to hope they were safe. "Is it over?"

"Not for you." The stranger's voice came from behind her.

Before she could turn around, a beefy hand grabbed her arm and yanked her hard to her feet. Her muscles seemed to tear as if she were made of paper. Blinding pain shot up to her shoulder and pounded there.

The pressure of the attacker's hand on her elbow made her vision blur. Nausea rolled over her, but she bit it back. She wanted to reach up and slap the man's gun away. It hovered right in front of her face, pointed at the dead center of Adam's chest.

Adam stood now, facing down the remaining gunman with his own weapon drawn. It was a standoff and suddenly it hurt just to stay on her feet.

"Let her go." Adam's voice dipped to a gravelly octave she'd never heard before.

A dark covering hid the gunman's face, but she could see the white teeth in his feral smile. "You messed up. You only counted two."

Adam's gaze never wavered. He stared the attacker down, looking every bit as terrifying as the man in battle gear. "I'm guessing there were three of you."

"Lower your weapon or I'll kill her."

"No."

The pain took her breath away as the dizziness assaulted her brain. "Adam—"

The attacker chuckled in a deep grumble that promised an unending nightmare of anguish. "Listen to her panic. Now imagine what I'll do to her before she dies."

"You need her alive."

"We're not negotiating."

She tried to focus on Adam, to send him a silent message that she was about to drop. But every time she blinked he shifted. It was subtle and the move so slight, but he now stood off to the left instead of directly in front of her.

And he kept talking. "That's the plan, right? You need to take her back to your boss."

"You don't have to worry about it since you'll be dead."

Adam shook his head, then shot the attacker a patronizing grin. "No."

She felt the gunman jerk. "What?"

Adam's smile grew wider. "Your turn."

"What are you—" With the gun blast the question turned to a gurgle. Blood spurted out of the man's neck as his hands dropped and his body fell right after.

Shock and disgust knocked her speechless. Not that this was her first body or even her first bloodbath. No, she'd earned her ticket into witness protection the hard way, through the deaths of others. Still, she stood there held together by nothing more than a bit of adrenaline and watched the red puddle inch closer to her once white sneakers.

Adam reached out but didn't touch her. "Maddie?"

"You could have killed me by accident."

"I've got good aim." Adam glanced around. "I think we're clear here."

Anger flooded through her and exploded, spewing with enough strength to break her. She clenched her jaw to keep from screaming him deaf. "You are supposed to be a computer guy."

"Sometimes I am."

His shrug just made her more furious. "What are you the rest of the time?"

"An agent with the Recovery Project."

"What the heck is that?"

"I work for Rod Lehman."

Just like that her anger evaporated. Melted right out of her. "Rod?"

"There are three things you need to know right now. Ready?" He didn't wait for a reply. "Rod's missing. You're in trouble. We have to go."

The pieces floated around in her mind, but she couldn't put them together. "I don't—"

"But first I have to fix your shoulder." Adam tucked his gun in his waistband. "This is going to hurt."

"What is?"

Before she could pull back or process what he planned to do, he bent her elbow at a ninety-degree angle then rotated her arm to the left then right. Each movement shot red-hot pain through her body. She cried out for him to stop as tears filled her eyes. When she couldn't take one more turn, something popped in her shoulder and the ruthless agony stopped.

She tried to catch her breath, but she could only pant and glare as she rubbed the spreading soreness. "What was that?"

"I fixed your dislocated shoulder."

She thought about strangling him with her good arm. "You killed two men—"

"Three."

She shifted to her right and glanced around him. The third body lay just feet away from the spot where Adam had curled up around her on the ground.

She stared at him again. "Were you shot?"

He looked offended by the question. "Of course not."

Massaging her injured shoulder made it throb even harder, so she stopped. "Right. How silly of me."

"And it's Wright."

She looked him over for signs of blood, wondering how a guy could take out three obviously trained killers and not suffer anything more than a wrinkled shirt. "Do you have a head injury or something?"

"The name is Adam Wright, not Wallace."

That little tidbit ticked her off. "And I'm just supposed to believe you?"

"Yes."

Her fury was ridiculous. She knew that. She lived under an assumed name with a life she never wanted and certainly didn't earn. She had no right to judge him. But now she understood she couldn't trust him and that ticked her off. He'd taken out a trio of guys with guns, but she still didn't know who was on what side.

And she could not depend on him to be honest. The only thing that saved him from a knee to the groin was the way he threw out Rod's name.

"Is anything about you real?" she asked.

"I could ask you the same thing."

Chapter Three

Luke Hathaway stepped up to the conference room table of the newly rebuilt Recovery Project headquarters. From the outside, the place looked like nothing more than an abandoned beige warehouse near the southwest Washington, D.C., waterfront. Inside was a different story.

Monitors and enough flashy electronic machinery to make even the most hardened technogeek smile lined one wall. Adam had set up the surveillance part of the office, using the unwanted inheritance of Luke's wife, Claire, to fund the construction.

Stairs ran up from the middle of the large open room to the crash-pad bedroom above. The space under the stairs served as both a storage space and an informal seating area with couches and chairs.

The building stayed in lockdown and required palm prints and a secret code for access. Luke insisted on the extra security measures after a group of commandos had stormed his suburban home and left in body bags.

Three months ago they'd operated as a quasi-governmental but still legitimate venture. They found missing people, both those who wanted rescue and those who were desperate to stay hidden. One of those missions had centered on Claire. Saving her had meant blowing their agency cover and losing their funding, all at the direction of a corrupt politician who had died in a shoot-out with Recovery agents.

Now they were a private organization, which meant no government oversight…and no one to stand up for them if they messed up. Since they rarely did, that was not much of a concern.

Luke took the seat at the head of the table and reached for the coffeepot in front of him. He poured what was his fourth cup before six in the morning. Much more and his eyes would float.

"What's the word from Adam?" he asked the others in the room.

Without any planning or fanfare, the team had designated Luke their interim leader now that Rod Lehman, the previous boss, had gone missing. Making the head chair the one available to Luke was their way of reaching a silent agreement on the matter. Their loyalty humbled him.

"Adam checked in. Said there was gunfire during the extraction." Caleb Mattern managed to fold his arms behind his head and shrug at the same time. "He took out three and is on the way back here with the Timmons woman."

Avery, Caleb's wife of one week, reached for a mug and settled into the chair across from her husband. They held matching science degrees and both excelled in forensics. The sly smile on her face said she was using her investigative skills now to eye up her spouse.

"It is amazing to me how you guys can say stuff like that and think it's normal," she said.

Caleb's mouth dropped open in mock surprise. "It's not?"

Luke enjoyed the banter, actually hated to break it up since the headquarters served as Caleb and Avery's temporary home. They deserved a place to step away from work, but they didn't have it right now.

Getting Avery to safety during their recent search for Rod had left Caleb's condo open to compromise. Their new place was being retrofitted with the appropriate security measures. Until Adam was satisfied the condo near the National Zoo had every precaution and a host of silent alarms, Caleb and Avery made their home above the stairs.

"Any chance Adam took care of the bodies before he got in the truck?" Luke asked once the couple went from bickering to staring at each other. Luke didn't want to get in the middle of that, either.

"I'll check." Caleb spun his chair around to face the bank of monitors and started typing on one of the keyboards. "But you know Adam."

"I'll assume that means no." Luke reached for the phone in the middle of the table.

Avery morphed from newlywed to concerned team member. She'd worked in a government lab, analyzing exhibits and evidence for criminal cases until she'd helped Recovery on an off-the-books job and got placed on administrative leave. That left all her attention for Recovery and Caleb.

"Do you think we need to send in reinforcements just in case Adam missed someone?" she asked.

Luke shook his head. "Never get there in

time. Besides, Adam was doing a grab and run. He should be long gone. It's pretty standard stuff."

Avery snorted. "Only if the grabee cooperates."

"How could any woman say no to Adam?" Caleb laughed at his own joke then grew serious. "The bigger question is, who sent the men? Taking out the crooked WitSec handler a month ago clearly didn't stop the bloodshed. That means, as we feared, this is not done."

"We could have more victims, more participants in the program whose locations are being given up for cash," Avery said.

"Exactly." That familiar anxiety churned in Luke's gut. "I want Adam back here so we can question the Timmons woman and figure out how to keep her hidden until we find the person at the head of this killing scheme."

Caleb yawned into his mug. "Now."

"What?"

"You mean, who's in charge now. So far we've already uncovered a conspiracy involving Bram Walters, a now very dead congressman, and a supervisor in the Marshals Service who handled WitSec participants."

Avery raised her hand. "Don't forget Trevor Walters."

Caleb swore under his breath. "Can't even though I want to."

"He's in on this. I can feel it. Being Bram's brother just increases the taint on Trevor as far as I can tell," she said.

Luke wished it were as easy as thinking it was true. "We have to prove it. Until we do, Trevor is just a very rich, very connected and very untouchable businessman."

"We'll get him."

Luke wanted to agree with Avery, but being sure about Trevor's involvement hadn't stopped the disaster so far. They needed facts and a way to take him out. "Try Adam again."

Caleb nodded. "Will do."

"How is Claire?" Avery's voice softened as she asked the question.

Just the mention of his wife's name and Luke felt the tension ease from his shoulders. "Pregnant and pissed because I insist she have security all the time."

Avery smiled. "This will all be over soon."

"Let's hope." Luke turned to Caleb. "What does Adam say?"

Caleb spun back around to face the table. His lips were thinned in a grim line. "Nothing. I suddenly can't reach him."

ADAM GOT MADDIE into his truck and watched her strap the seat belt across her chest. She stayed quiet and agreed with everything he said, followed every direction without fighting back. Didn't try to kick him or steal his weapon.

He didn't buy the act for one second. He'd bet his life she was waiting for the right time to run.

He wanted to think his sound arguments had convinced her to calm down, but he knew that wasn't true. This woman was trained by Rod, the same man who'd trained Adam. She wouldn't believe a stranger who showed up to pull her out of bed and race through the woods. She wouldn't admit to being in WitSec.

And she wouldn't sit quietly in his truck while he drove her to some unknown destination.

She was not stupid. She possessed street smarts and a stunning will to live. Turning evidence on a boyfriend who ran the biggest meth operation in Chicago proved that. Maddie was smart enough to get out and cut a deal with the Justice Department, one that landed her in WitSec and eventually in his lap.

Adam just hoped she'd put her drug past behind her. He didn't want to deal with her going through withdrawal or looking for a hit. Recovery had a no-drug policy. They were all clean and no one questioned it. Adam believed in getting his thrills in other ways. Always had.

"Russell Ambrose is dead." Adam meant to deliver the news of her handler with a little less anger in his voice and a whole lot more tact, but it didn't work out that way.

Her head whipped around. Her unblinking stare out the window ended that fast. "What?"

He slipped the keys into the ignition but didn't start the car. "He was giving away the identities of WitSec participants. He collected cash and got them killed."

When she just stared at him, Adam rushed to fill the uncomfortable silence. "That's why I'm here."

"To kill me."

"No." He shook his head for emphasis since words alone didn't appear to be working.

"Sure feels like it."

"Maddie, listen to me. I'm trying to help you."

"Right. Because the bad guys always admit they're trying to kill you." Sarcasm dripped from her voice.

"Good point." He turned the key. "I know about Rod."

"I don't know who that is."

Looked as if they were back to denial. Adam wasn't surprised, but he was getting frustrated. "I can tell you anything from your file."

She folded and refolded her hands on her lap. "I don't know what you're talking about."

He hit the door locks just in case she ended the innocent act and headed for the handle to escape. "I know you're trained to pretend. I get that."

"Call the police."

She could have told him she was a toaster oven and he would have been less surprised. He admired the move. It shoved him right into a corner. "I don't think so."

"If what you're saying is true, call the police." She glanced around the truck. "I don't have a phone but I'm betting you do and I know you're smart enough to dial 911."

He did have a phone, but the real power came from his watch. It was how he communicated with the other agents, and that was the least impressive of its functions. "Taking you in will send a message to someone in WitSec.

A handler will come to pick you up and hush up everything with the police."

"Exactly."

"I can't risk it."

"Neither can I." She launched her body in his direction as she unlatched her seat belt.

If he hadn't been expecting the attack she would have slammed his head against the window. Even waiting for it, she got in a few good shots.

She grabbed for the keys with one hand and punched him in the jaw with the other. The hit sent his head back. The smack against the headrest hurt his neck more than the blow, but she didn't let up. Her fists pummeled his legs and chest.

When she switched to scratching, dragging her fingers across his forearm until she drew blood, he went from defense to an offensive strike. He grabbed her hand and leaned hard against her, pinning her on her back against the seat.

Her knee caught him in the stomach as she squirmed and flailed. She grunted and panted, forcing him to use more strength than he intended. He'd hoped to talk her down. That was before she aimed for his groin.

"Maddie, stop."

"You're hurting me."

That admission ripped through him. He hated the idea of giving her so much as a bruise. "Stop trying to run and I'll get up."

He doubled his intent, stretching her arms above her head and straddling her upper thighs. He braced one foot on the floor and leaned over her, his face just inches from hers. He tried to get her to look at him, but she rolled her head from side to side, her neck muscles straining as she tried to knock him to the floor.

"Get off me." She lifted her hips in an attempt to buck him off then let out a shriek.

The high-pitched sound echoed in his ears. "What is it?"

"Nothing." The word came out through staccato breaths.

He recognized pain when he saw it. He figured he had to be hurting her sore shoulder and tried to adjust his hold. "Better?"

"No."

"Margaret Thomas."

At the mention of the name she stopped pushing and mumbling. Her chest rose and fell in a rapid pace he feared would stop her heart.

But he had her attention. "That's your real

name. You grew up in Indiana, the only child of Frank and Louise. Your father died when you were fourteen. Your mother died last year, but you couldn't go to the funeral because of the program's rules."

Maddie bit her lip but stayed quiet.

"You testified against Knevin Leonard, your boyfriend and partner in a drug ring. He vowed to kill you for turning him in. Even hired some nasty guys to try it."

"No."

The truth was written all over her face, from the sadness in her eyes to the tightening of the skin over her cheekbones. "Yes."

"You're wrong."

"Maddie, please." He had to break through her protective shield. He had about an hour's drive to headquarters. He couldn't spend every moment worrying she'd leap through the window if he slowed down to change lanes. "I can tell you where you met Rod the first time. Would that convince you?"

"I wasn't his partner."

Adam sat back, resting his weight on his knees and his hands on his thighs. " I don't understand."

She slowly lowered her arms. "I never dealt drugs and didn't know Knevin was doing it."

For whatever reason, it seemed that was the one piece of information she couldn't tolerate being told. Didn't matter that the evidence said otherwise, she was sticking with the innocence story on that one.

It wasn't his business. She could tell whatever lie she needed to tell to wrestle the guilt away from her bed at night. But disappointment still pounded him. He'd invested so much time in watching over her that he wanted her to at least own up to her mistakes. They all had a few. Sure, hers were bigger than most, but that just made her human.

He shook off the anger before it could fester. "Fine."

"You don't believe me."

"I don't care." But he did. The idea of her getting drugs into kids' hands gnawed at him. Made him want to shake her until she promised never to fall back into those habits.

The emotion washed out of her face, leaving behind only a blank stare. "What happens now?"

"Same plan." He sat back in his seat and held a hand out to help her up. "We go to the Recovery Project headquarters until we can figure out a way to keep you safe."

She ignored his offer and sat up on her own.

The process took longer than usual for such an easy activity. She twisted and winced.

"And I'm supposed to ignore protocol and not call my handler?"

"Ambrose is dead."

"So you keep saying." She tried to turn around and face front then stilled. Adam thought if she bit down any harder on her lower lip, she'd chew right through it.

"Is it your shoulder?"

She stretched, grimacing with every move. "No."

"It's something. "

She bent over with her elbows on her knees and inhaled several deep breaths. "I thought you were the smart guy who knew my file."

He searched his memory but couldn't come up with anything to explain the green cast to her skin. "Meaning?"

"If you were, you'd know about my back."

An old injury. That explained it. His intel was incomplete, didn't reach back much further than the trial prep and police file. It was hard enough even getting that much since her identity was tightly protected. "What about it?"

"I broke it."

Her shoulder had to be throbbing and now

her back. Guilt racked him. He could have been more careful. Maybe not when the gunmen were firing, but certainly when he was trying to get her to listen to him. "When?"

She looked up at him. "When my former boyfriend threw me off a building."

Chapter Four

Trevor Walters leaned back in his chair and stared at the man sitting on the other side of his desk. If Trevor had his way, John Tate would disappear. Just step into a hole in the earth and never be seen again. It was tempting to make that happen.

If John were a different man, one with less powerful friends and a less visible career, he'd be gone. His pseudowealth and puffed-up overconfidence wouldn't save him.

The man had all the obvious trappings Trevor despised. Everything about John screamed poor taste wrapped up in a bundle of new money. Passable suit. Shiny watch. Big government title. And not a clue about the danger he invited into his world when he came up against Trevor.

John was the deputy director of the Justice Department's Office of Enforcement Operations. He handled intricate government surveillance and held all the power in the witness protection program, including having the final say on who got in and who didn't.

But Trevor was more concerned with the man's side job: newly minted blackmailer. That was the position that would get John killed. Trevor vowed to make that true.

"I have to wonder where you got the men to fight this particular battle against the Recovery Project," Trevor said.

"Why?"

"Seems they were not very successful against Adam Wright and Maddie Timmons. One could say they were ill prepared for what they found in West Virginia."

"This time."

Trevor predicted the answer was more like every time. "I would have thought you would ask to use my men."

Not that he would have agreed. Orion Industries was his baby, a legitimate government-contracts firm he built from nothing. The business specialized in threat management, whether that meant assisting fledgling foreign governments or working for his own. He was not about to ruin Orion's stellar reputation by dragging it into John's mess.

"I didn't realize you'd been successful fighting the Recovery Team agents." John made a show of brushing something off his charcoal dress pants. "From what I remember, every time you've gone against Recovery you've had to make up a story about an accident in training exercises and call your men's next of kin. That's not exactly a stellar history either, now, is it?"

Not that Trevor needed a reminder of that fact. His losses had been high enough for him to enter into an informal deal with Luke Hathaway, Recovery's leader: Trevor would leave Recovery alone and vice versa. After all, there were only so many men on his payroll qualified and trustworthy enough to do the dirty off-the-books job and he was running low.

But John didn't know any of that and Trevor was not about to fill him in. "I am smart enough not to full-on fight with Recovery, but if I did I assure you I would most definitely succeed."

John smiled. "I wonder if your brother counted on that fact."

Trevor curled his fingers into fists to keep from reaching for the gun taped under his desk. "Leave Bram out of this."

"Why? The Recovery agents killed him."

John smacked his lips together in mock concern. "I still don't understand why you've refrained from seeking revenge."

"Because I am civilized?"

"You could have unloaded. Bram was, after all, a highly respected congressman. At least in the public's view. Though we know better, don't we?"

Trevor had kept the real circumstances of Bram's death quiet to preserve his brother's legacy. Trevor hoped the Walters brothers' involvement with the WitSec money-for-information scheme would end at Bram's grave.

It might have if John hadn't gotten his hands on the tape that changed Trevor's life. That made him a target instead of a leader. "Maybe you should focus your attention on keeping your moneymaking plan quiet instead of on my private life."

"But that's why you're here, isn't it?"

John never did have grasp of the obvious. "You happen to be in my office."

"This time." John's mouth twisted in a snarl as he said the words. "I won't tolerate being ordered around again."

But he would. Trevor would make John do it over and over until Trevor got bored with the cat-and-mouse game.

"I will do what I have to do until you realize you do not own me."

"But I do…unless you want a certain tape to go public."

Trevor mentally pledged to redouble his efforts to get that tape. If he couldn't find it, he'd do things the hard way. Maybe start with John's pretty little wife.

Trevor would have a file on her by morning. "It is interesting how a man who has sold out WitSec particpants' locations for cash is trying to use blackmail and threats of public-image destruction to get his way."

"Nothing in those deaths points to me. Since the identities were secret, the deaths aren't even public knowledge. No one knows to investigate the losses, such as they are."

"Interesting."

It appeared John was not smart enough to realize every conversation in the office was recorded. Even his underling Russell Ambrose got that, and Russell was dumb enough to get himself killed at the Recovery agents' feet.

The public didn't know why Russell died in a shoot-out for fear the news of a witness handler selling information would upend the program, but powerful people in government now knew. A top-secret investigation into

WitSec was all but assured, which Trevor assumed was why John wanted the loose ends tied and tucked.

"I will concede the men I sent to retrieve Ms. Timmons failed in their quest," John said.

"Apparently."

John leaned forward, his smarmy self-satisfaction abandoned in favor of fevered whispers. "We cannot afford to have her welcomed into the protective bosom of the Recovery Project."

"We?"

"She is with one of their agents."

Adam Wright. Trevor knew all about him. About all the agents. "I have read the intel on your failed mission. I know the facts."

"Then you know we are at a turning point."

Trevor could smell the desperation on the other man. The weakness disgusted him. "Meaning?"

"You need to step up and play your part."

Trevor shifted in his chair. The leather felt comfortable again now that he was back in control and his unwanted guest was squirming. "This conversation would work better if you would stop talking in wild generalities and asking rhetorical questions."

"You need to terminate Adam Wright and Maddie Timmons."

"That will just bring the entire Recovery team to my doorstep. No, thank you."

"Then kill them all."

Just when Trevor thought John could not get more reckless, he did. "I think law enforcement would notice a mass murder within the D.C. metro area."

"Then you better be careful in how you do it. I'd suggest a gas explosion."

"Subtle."

"Something believable that will take them all out."

Trevor exhaled to show his displeasure with the ridiculous conversation. "The Recovery team is made up of law enforcement officers of sorts. Former military, maybe, but still, they have friends in high places."

John jumped to his feet. "Then you pick something. Just get it done."

MADDIE RECHARGED BY THE TIME Adam drove through the thick metal gate surrounding the beat-up beige warehouse. The thought of being locked inside the premises sent a rush of panic through every cell and pore in her body. Her innate tendency to run to safety and ask questions later kicked into gear. It took all her control to sit there and let Adam usher her into the unknown.

She figured if he wanted her dead he would have killed her by now. She repeated the refrain until it took hold and she started to believe it.

"I don't want to kill you," Adam said in what could only be described as a you've-got-to-be-kidding tone.

She had to smile. "I guess I said that out loud, huh?"

He threw her a sidelong glance. "Yeah."

"Can you blame me?"

"No."

She expected him to defend his position and argue his case. By agreeing, he sucked the heat right out of her. Still, she needed to follow protocol. Her handlers had drummed the plan into her head until it played in her dreams. Get to a safe place and call. She couldn't promise on the first, but she could make the second happen.

Let Adam explain to the U.S. Marshals Service why she was safer with him when they broke down the doors to rescue her. She just needed to stay safe. She'd fought too hard, sacrificed too much, to risk it all over a sexy man with an even sexier dimple.

Adam parked and nearly broke a speed record coming around to her side of the truck to open the door. He likely thought she would bolt. Since he'd driven into a secure and brightly lit garage, a place with few obvious exits, he didn't have to worry. Even she wouldn't try to break her way through a metal wall.

"How are you feeling?" His voice dipped low as he asked the question.

The sexy vibration made her insides jump around in excitement. "Fine."

He lifted an eyebrow. "Maddie."

She rolled her eyes. "The shoulder and the back hurt."

"We can get you some medical attention."

"You won't call the police but you'll call an ambulance?"

"I think he means me." A guy slipped in behind Adam. "Hey, man. Have a nice time in West Virginia?"

She tensed but Adam smiled. "Maddie, this is Caleb Mattern."

"I work with Adam," Caleb explained as he held out his hand toward her.

She shook the man's hand and then pulled

hers back fast. She wasn't even out of the truck and she had to battle two of them.

And what exactly did these guys eat? Caleb stood over six feet, with broad shoulders, light brown hair and the most soothing blue-green eyes she'd ever seen. He had that handsome mussed look that reminded her of blue jeans and football on Sunday afternoons. The relaxed style matched his welcoming smile. The only surprise was the shiny gold wedding band.

Attractive or not, she didn't trust Caleb one inch more than she trusted Adam. Well, that wasn't true. She reluctantly believed Adam wanted to help her. She didn't know why or if her radar was off, but she was willing to go along for now. But only with Adam.

"I hear you got banged up," Caleb said.

She'd been with Adam every single minute since the attackers came. He hadn't made a call. She'd know, since she'd been watching for a cell phone so she could steal it. "Who told you that?"

"It's on the radio." Adam frowned at her in a way that said he thought she was clueless. "How do you think? I did."

"When?"

Adam waved her off then reached up to drag her out of the truck. "Don't worry about it."

She wasn't in the mood to be placated or manhandled. She pulled out of his reach and ignored Caleb's half cough, half laugh as she did. "You want me to trust you but you're keeping information from me. How is that fair?"

Caleb crossed his arms over his chest. "She's got you there, man."

"Don't help."

Caleb's smile grew wider. "Can't seem to stop."

"She can fight her own battles."

Caleb nodded. "I get it. I've been there."

"Where?" Maddie asked.

Adam glared as his teammate for about ten seconds before turning back to her. "I used my watch."

Maddie didn't follow. Maybe she did need a bed and an aspirin before she could function again. "What does that mean?"

Adam held out his wrist to her. "It works like a telephone only better."

The black face looked like most other watches but bigger. She could see a series of buttons and when Adam hit one, the face switched to an image of the garage.

Caleb pointed around the space. "Cameras. You're almost never alone here."

She was more interested in the phone part. "Where can I get one of those?"

"Adam designed this one. We all wear them."

With all the gunfire and running, she'd almost forgotten about the other side of him. "So, the computer-geek thing is real."

"I prefer the word *genius*."

Adam exhaled. "I'm sure you do."

Caleb didn't try to hide his laugh that time. "Let's take this discussion inside."

He reached in the cab to bring her out. Instinctively, she shrank back, wedging her body into the seat. When Caleb stared at her with a she's-nuts-and-getting-crazier-by-the-second look all men did so well, she sat back up.

"Sorry," she mumbled.

Caleb winked. "It takes more than that to offend me, but I do want to make sure you're okay."

She didn't want to like them, either of them. Caleb made her feel comfortable. Adam made her all tingly. She didn't care for either reaction.

"You're a doctor?" she asked.

"I'm the forensics and science guy on the

team. We all have emergency training, but mine is a bit more extensive."

Yeah, no, thanks. "I'm fine."

"You don't have a choice, Maddie. I insist."

When Adam said things like that, got all dictatorial and grumpy, she didn't like him much at all. "Insist?"

"We are done running and hiding, and you need someone to look you over. It can either be Caleb or me. Choose."

She dug her nails into her palms. "Oh, really."

"You're safe here, and that's the last time I'm going to tell you that."

Caleb cleared his throat. "It might be more believable if you weren't yelling at her."

Adam's voice got louder. "I tried being nice—"

That was news to her. "When?"

"We have questions and she's going to answer them." Adam put his hand under her elbow. The gentle touch contrasted with his gruff words.

She slid out of the seat and glanced up at Caleb's smiling face. "Do you have another team member I can talk to?"

He nodded. "Sure."

Adam talked over both of them. "Nice try, but you're stuck with me."

That's exactly what had her worried.

Chapter Five

Trevor called in the one person he knew he could trust. With his position, that list was short. Everyone wanted something from him but would abandon him for a better deal if offered.

His vice presidents were loyal to the company so long as their paychecks kept coming. Trevor was not simple enough to confuse career security with friendship. The men he employed to work those "special" side jobs were even more of a question mark. They stuck around for the adrenaline high and consistent wire transfers. That didn't mean they wouldn't sell him out if it meant their freedom versus his.

His confidants used to include his wife until she dumped their marriage without warning and waited until they'd divided their property to threaten to take their son away. She had money thanks to their divorce and counted on his need to keep her happy and quiet. She knew enough to make her a serious threat.

Despite their custody agreement, she'd run to the media and questioned his competency to co-parent and his influence on their child. That was when he made the biggest mistake of his life.

He asked the wrong person the wrong question about getting rid of a wife. Russell Ambrose. And Ambrose took advantage of the situation to drag Bram and Trevor into the WitSec disaster. Now John had the evidence, the blackmail fodder and a mistaken belief he could control the situation.

Well, that soon would end.

"Did you need to see me?" Sela Andrews, his young and very capable assistant, peeked around the door.

He waved to her. "Come in."

"Of course." With a notepad in her hands, she shut the door and walked across the carpeted office to stand on the opposite side of his desk.

He took in her tight skirt and long legs. If the tape was his dumbest move all year then she was his smartest. She had wavy blond hair and a smile, both sexy and sweet, that sent even his strongest competitor into a babbling tailspin.

She'd fallen on hard times early in her business career, before Trevor rushed in and picked her up. He gave her a purpose and she repaid him with unquestioning loyalty.

"I need some information," he said.

She flipped through a few pages. "For which contract?"

"This is a personal issue."

"I see."

"We know the Recovery Project is back in business and the general location of its new headquarters. The search of tax and real-estate records hasn't uncovered the exact address." Once again Trevor had to tip his hat to Luke Hathaway. The man was a worthy adversary. "Luke hid this one well. Probably had some technical help from Adam and possibly assistance from old government contacts who think Recovery got a raw deal."

"We just need a street address?"

"We need to narrow it down to the building, get a schematic and some idea of the firepower and technical abilities they have there." When she didn't balk or show any reaction except interest, he continued. "Security, alarms, I need everything I can get, but it all starts with an address."

"Should I ask the Technical Department—"

"No one knows about the particulars of this one but us."

She frowned. "I don't understand."

"I'm going to set up a private meeting with Luke." Sela knew all about the Recovery Project. She was the only one other than Trevor to touch the paperwork and see the files he had on the Project. "I need someone tracking him from that point forward. Eventually he'll lead us to the right building. I'll take it from there."

Trevor usually stuck to administration, but he would make an exception. He hadn't built the business by sitting on his butt. He could shoot and conduct surveillance. Nowadays he had the luxury of delegating, but he hadn't lost the skills.

"But that means I have to tell someone to get started," she said.

"True." He wrote a name down on a piece of paper. His second-in-command of security and a guy who understood the importance of a dollar and not asking questions. "Call him on his private line. He will not need to know why he's following Luke. Just get him photos of the agents, tell him to keep his distance and call me with a report."

"Right." She turned back to the door.

"And, Sela?"

She glanced at him over her shoulder. "Yes?"

"He can't get caught."

ADAM LOOKED AROUND the table at his friends, the men he trusted more than anyone else in the world. They worked together, laughed together, drank together and suffered together.

He wanted to punch them.

Every single one of them had worn a stupid grin since he'd brought Maddie in. He knew what was happening. One by one they'd peeled off and gotten married, or in Holden's case, engaged. Zach remained single, but it was hard to imagine a guy who barely spoke finding a woman who would tolerate him forever.

But the woman thing was like an infectious disease with this group. Once one of them walked down the aisle, some silent torch was passed, and Adam had no interest in taking a turn.

Not that he didn't love women. He loved them in general and specifically he loved Claire, Mia and Avery for what they brought into the lives of Luke, Holden and Caleb. But that didn't mean he intended to take his own fall. He'd been there and was still recovering from the fallout of Robyn's death five years ago. Losing one girlfriend in such a shocking and sudden way was all he would ever accept.

He stood behind Maddie's chair now and pointed around the conference table, adding a glare with each introduction. "Luke Hathaway, weapons expert and leader. Holden Price, tactics and strategy. And Caleb you met. He's not worth a second round of hellos."

Caleb saluted Adam with his coffee mug. "Thanks, man."

Adam held up a salute of a different kind. "The only missing member is Zach Bachman."

"Zach's the one who likes to blow things up." Holden sent Maddie a smile as he spoke. He flirted and won women over without even trying.

Maddie seemed bored by it all, but her hands told a different story. She twirled the coffee mug between her fingers, letting it clank against the table with each turn. "Is this Zach guy off kidnapping another woman or is that Adam's specialty?"

Caleb laughed. "I like her."

Adam refused to be won over that easily.

This woman had a complicated past. And he wasn't interested…mostly. "I'm sure she's thrilled to know that."

"Zach is at my house with my wife, Claire, and Caleb's wife, Avery." Luke poured another cup of coffee and downed half of it in one gulp.

"And the woman Holden hopes will one day suffer a brain injury and marry him," Adam said.

Holden snorted. "He means my fiancée, Mia."

Maddie blew out a long breath. "That's a lot of people to keep track of."

Adam reached over her shoulder and grabbed her mug. "And here's the main point—none of us are trying to kill you."

Holden frowned. "Adam, what the—"

"She can't figure out if we're good guys or not. I'm trying to convince her and thought maybe repetition would help."

Maddie waved her hands in front of her. "The fact that I don't automatically believe Adam upsets him."

"Forgive him. He's not so good with women," Caleb said.

"Apparently," she mumbled.

Adam pulled out the chair next to Maddie

and sat down. "Can we get back to the debriefing?"

"Is that what this is?" Maddie looked around the table. "If so, you're going to be disappointed."

"Why?" Luke asked.

"I'm not an oversharer. I'm not about to spill every detail and tell you all about my life. Just let me confirm everything with Rod and get his opinion—"

Luke shook his head. "Can't."

It was Adam's turn to sigh. "I'm pretty sure I already explained this."

She stopped glancing around and focused on him. "Try again."

It still hurt to say the words. Adam had used every search he could think of, tapped into every resource. He'd hacked into intelligence databases and the private files of every person he could trace to Rod. And found nothing.

Adam swallowed back the fear something had happened to Rod and the horrible suspicion nothing had. Both scenarios kept him from sleeping more than four hours in a row. "Rod uncovered the problem in WitSec. He gathered information and then disappeared. We tracked you down from the notations in one of his files. We couldn't piece together much except your name."

"I don't really understand," she said.

"Rod realized that someone had sold the new names and addresses of at least three woman in witness protection to people who were willing to pay big money for the details. Bad people." Adam wasn't sure how she'd react to this part so he rushed through it to get it over with. "Someone on the inside, or a group of people, profited while two of these women were tracked down and killed."

She visibly swallowed. "And the third?"

"You," Luke said.

She glanced around the table, her mouth falling straighter as she went. "You're sure?"

"Your name was on Rod's list but it's the part where three guys just tried to kill us in West Virginia that confirmed it for me." Adam had the rocking headache as further proof.

"You said Rod had the information and now he's gone. So, how did you put all the other stuff together?" Her voice turned softer as the sentence continued.

Adam looked at Luke for guidance. When he shook his head, Adam knew not to mention David Brennan's name. The guy had been a congressional staffer at the time, but he'd won the special election and now was Representative Brennan. "From our contact in a congressional office."

Luke leaned forward and grabbed the coffeepot again. "Bram Walters had your personal file locked away somewhere. Not sure how he got it, but the guy was crooked. Who knows how he did anything."

Her mouth dropped open. "The congressman who died saving the woman who worked for him…?"

"I see the lady knows her news," Caleb said.

She looked around the table until her gaze stopped on Holden. "Wait a minute."

"Yeah, that was Mia, my fiancée, and Walters didn't save her. He tried to kill her."

Caleb nodded. "So we killed him."

Maddie made a hissing sound. "This is a lot to take in."

Adam thought her eyes might explode. They were huge and glassy and the confusion on her face was tough to miss. He sympathized.

He couldn't exactly blame her. If he hadn't been working on the inside, uncovering the conspiracy, he never would have been able to follow along. Or believe.

Looked as if he'd handed her another reason

to doubt him. "You've only heard part of it, but you get the idea."

She brushed her hand through her long hair. "So, where is Rod now?"

"We can't find him. No leads, no forensics, no credit card or alias usage. It's like he disappeared." The words sliced into Adam as he said them.

He excelled at tracking people and for some reason he couldn't find the only person he wanted to see. The failure filled him with a fury that tried to claw its way out.

For the first time since he met her, Maddie smiled. "Like me."

Luke choked on his mouthful of coffee. "You're saying you think Rod is now in the program?"

She shrugged. "The scenario sounds familiar."

"No." Adam refused to believe that. "Rod would figure out a way to let us know."

Her smile faded. "If you say so."

"He would."

"I didn't and believe me I wanted to." She looked over at Luke. "Were there others? More than the two WitSec women who were killed, I mean."

Luke hesitated for a second before replying. "Only the three of you that we know of, but there could be more. We only have Rod's cryptic notes and who knows if he uncovered everyone in this thing."

She pushed back from the table, holding her arms stiff in front of her as if preparing for a verbal deathblow. "So, who's trying to kill me and why?"

"We're guessing your ex paid big money to…uh…" Holden sputtered to a halt. He just sat there.

"Make me disappear."

"Yes." Adam didn't see a reason to pretty it up. This woman could take bad news. She'd had more than her share in her twenty-eight years.

"Knevin paid to get the information so he could kill me." Her hands shook. "This is his revenge."

Adam nodded. "That's the way it looks. Knevin paid for your info. Other people paid for the other women's info."

Maddie let her head fall back. She stared up at the ceiling with her fingers clenched onto the wooden table in front of her. "He's just turned out to be the gift that keeps on giving."

Her anguish ate at Adam. Despite the crimes

that had landed her in this position, the instinct to protect her rose out of nowhere and slapped him.

He reached over and brushed his palm over her forearm. "If it's any consolation, we're impressed you turned him in. Entering the program is not easy."

Her muscles relaxed as she settled back into her seat. "Or all that stable, since my first handler is missing and Adam tells me my recent one turned bad and is now dead."

"Admittedly, the program needs a review and overhaul," Luke said with a huge dose of humor in his voice.

Maddie must have picked up on the lighter mood because she shot Luke an apologetic look. "True, but I'm still not talking."

Adam looked at his fellow agents. "Told you."

"I don't have any information that could help you anyway."

Luke leaned in even farther as if trying to will her to talk. "You don't know that."

"Trust me." She smiled. "After all, isn't that what you're all expecting me to do with you?"

Chapter Six

Maddie didn't like the sleeping arrangements. She got the bed and the comforter. Adam got the couch downstairs. Poor Caleb and Avery got kicked over to Luke's house.

Maddie appreciated the game of musical beds for her benefit, but she needed the spot downstairs. The one closer to the telephones. She'd even hidden the painkillers Caleb given her for her back. She needed her wits. Dozing off before dawn and without making the necessary call wasn't an option, no matter how much she wanted it to be.

And she did. She didn't pretend to understand the agents she'd met but she couldn't help but like them. Whether they were torturing Adam with jokes or arguing about how to proceed, she saw the companionship. Envied it.

She'd never really had that certain closeness

with anyone but her mom. Missing her funeral was the one moment that could smash Maddie's control and reduce her to tears.

She couldn't grieve or apologize. Couldn't be there for support or explain how her life had gone so wrong so early and so stunningly fast. Knevin stole those precious moments that mattered more than her safety.

Throwing her off a building wasn't the worst thing he'd done to her. Robbing her of her life was. Those scars didn't heal or the pain abate with the right combination of pills and lotions. No amount of self-medicating could take away the suffocating guilt.

She looked at the chronic pain in her lower back as her penance. Some days she had trouble walking. After a long shift at the diner, she would soak in an ice bath just to function again.

Having Adam tackle her, even if it was to save her, wrenched something low and tenuous. Right now sitting had her gasping.

So, not taking the meds Caleb handed to her had taken every last ounce of strength she had. Getting down the stairs without waking Adam was no picnic, either. With her hand on the railing, she stepped as lightly as possible, placing each foot carefully and ignoring the agony that shot up her leg. The careful navigation had sweat beading on her forehead and her arm muscles shaking from fatigue.

When she finally hit the bottom riser, she exhaled, letting the air shudder out of her on a long sigh. Forcing her hand to unclench from the metal handrail took longer. She balanced there, listening to the hum of the machinery and soft buzz of the safety lighting in the kitchen area.

Now it was just a short walk to one of two options—the door or a phone. She knew she should leave. She'd seen Adam punch in the code. They all did when they left and no one had tried to hide it from her. It appeared getting in was the tough part. Exiting should be easier.

But she didn't want to go. Not that way. Sneaking out like a coward didn't appeal to her. After all the agents had done to help her, to make her feel welcome, she couldn't bolt without a word. She owed them more than that.

She knew Adam expected her to run. He believed the worst of her, that she'd dealt drugs and stood back not caring about the consequences. She was guilty of a lot of things but not that sin. No one could lay that at her feet.

The phone. She'd call and let her handler guide her actions from there, no matter what they were. She knew that amounted to abdicating responsibility, but the weight of maturity pressed her down to the point of crushing her. She needed a break.

Tiptoeing was out of the question, but she could silently slide across the hard floor. With slow and unsteady steps, she made her way to the computer monitors. She picked up the receiver. Instead of an insistent buzz, silence greeted her. She clicked on the button to disconnect but the noise didn't change. Figuring the phone was somehow hooked into the computer system and under Adam's control, she regrouped.

With the hand of her good arm wrapped around the back of a chair, she eased into the kitchen area. The phone there would be for an outside line. It had to be.

She barely had the handle off the cradle when the quiet hit her. This one didn't work, either. She spun around, almost falling to the floor in the process. There had to be a cell phone around there somewhere.

Her gaze ran all over the room…and stopped on the two men standing at the bottom of the staircase.

One she'd never seen before. He wore jeans and had short brown, almost military-style hair. The most unsettling part was his brown-eyed gaze. He stared right through her as if he could read her every thought.

The angry one pushing up his glasses was Adam. The gray sweatpants and slim white T-shirt highlighted every muscle, but did nothing to soften the harsh lines of his face.

"Looking for something?" Adam asked.

When nothing smart popped into her head, she went with her fallback option. "Getting a drink of water."

The mystery guy nodded toward the monitors. "We don't keep the drinking glasses in the computers."

She could keep up the pretense or just come clean. Since fooling the wall of testosterone looming in front of her would not be an easy feat, she threw out a little attitude of her own. "You cut the phone lines."

"Nothing so drastic," Adam said.

As usual, he answered with a non-answer. "Tell me."

He walked across the floor to stand in front of her. "When you picked up the phones they automatically went dead."

The other man joined them. "And sent an alarm to his watch."

"You are…?" She thought she knew but wanted to confirm her theory.

"Zach Bachman."

"The explosives guy."

"That's me."

"Happen to have a cell phone on you I could borrow, Zach?"

He shot her a crooked smile. "Sorry."

"That makes two of us," she mumbled.

"You're injured," Adam said, stating the obvious.

Truth was, her left leg kept tingling. The misfiring nerves would soon twist until the pain became unbearable. "I know that."

Zach's unreadable expression turned to one of concern. "What happened?"

"Someone threw her off a building."

Zach's concern morphed to fury. "In West Virginia?"

"Years ago," she explained.

Zach blinked. "You guys lost me."

"One bad guy dislocated her shoulder and another messed up her back." Adam shifted and ducked, wrapping his arm around her waist until he balanced her body against his.

Zach still looked lost. "Are either of these guys you?"

"No." Adam was barely paying attention to his friend. All his energy seemed focused on her and making sure she sat down.

It worked. With her good arm around his shoulders and her feet only skimming the floor, the waves of pain subsided. Letting Adam take on most of her weight took all the pressure away.

"Where were you going?" he asked as he guided her to the couch under the stairs and the tangle of sheets where he was supposed to be sleeping.

"I didn't try to leave, if that's what you're getting at." It was important to her that he knew that. She didn't know why, but she wanted it out there.

"Only because you were smart enough to know I'd rig the door to make that impossible."

She didn't know that before but she did now. "I need to check in with the program."

He lowered her to the cushion with a gentleness she didn't expect from a man with arms the size of small cars. He tucked the pillows in around her.

And never stopped lecturing. "You need to stay alive."

"Adam, please stop."

"Listen." He stood over her with his arms crossed and tension spilling out of him. "I can't bring Rod here, but I can come close."

She wanted to lean back and relax, but the comment brought her back to sanity. "What does that mean?"

"Rod's former partner, Vince Ritter."

Zach stepped up. "I'm not sure that's a good idea."

"Why?" she asked.

Adam stared at his friend. "That's what I'm wondering."

"We need to keep her location under wraps until we know who is trying to kill her." Zach's voice stayed even, but he focused so intensely on Adam he seemed to will his partner to understand.

The entire scene made her wary. Zach knew something. He had a piece of information that even Adam didn't appear to know. If they weren't going to share with each other, how could she trust them to open up to her?

She cut through the nonverbal battle between Adam and Zach and got right to the obvious conclusion. "You don't trust Vince."

Zach shook his head. "I didn't say that."

He didn't have to. "Is there anyone you guys do trust?"

He frowned at her. "Each other."

Adam nodded.

She closed her eyes wondering if they actually did.

ADAM SERIOUSLY CONSIDERED sitting guard all night on the bottom step. There weren't any reachable windows, but Maddie clearly had no boundaries, so he had to take drastic measures.

Zach stopped in front of him and handed over the extra beer in his hand. "You look like you could use this."

Adam took off his glasses and rubbed his eyes. "It's two in the morning."

"Your point?"

"Right." Adam took the bottle and tapped it against Zach's before moving over to make room on the stair.

"What's the thing about her being thrown off a building?"

Adam couldn't get the idea out of his head. It kept replaying until his stomach clenched and his back teeth ground together. He tried to imagine the sheer panic she must have felt before she went over. The pain once she woke up. She was damn lucky to be alive.

He wanted that Knevin creature dead. Preferably thrown off the roof of the prison and left to rot in twisted agony just so he'd understand the message.

It wasn't the first time fantasies of revenge ran through Adam's head. Years ago he'd stood by Robyn's grave, oblivious to the chill of the Portland rain, and vowed eternal hatred of all drunk drivers.

The tragedy changed the course of his life. Made him turn from computers to guns. Now, with Maddie, was the first time he felt sympathy for someone who dealt in mind-numbing false avenues that stole the lives of so many.

Maddie should be his enemy, someone he helped out of a sense of obligation, not desire. She should be nothing more than a job. But that hadn't been true since the second week in West Virginia. He watched her work long hours and treat everyone with a smile. Saw her fight for her life in the woods. She was a survivor and he was far too interested in getting to know the real woman behind the false identity.

"I don't know the details of the injury."

Adam picked at the label on his bottle. "Maddie is not talking."

"Did you try asking?" He exhaled, not wanting to say the words that would cause Zach to view Maddie as a criminal.

"She ran drugs. Her boyfriend was an—"

"She did not run drugs."

That was not the response Adam expected. Especially not so adamantly spoken. Not from Zach, a guy who rarely raised his voice. He almost shouted the denial.

Adam peeked around the staircase to make sure Maddie still slept on his place on the couch. She hadn't moved. Amazing what painkillers could do for an injury.

"You're the expert on her now?" Adam asked.

"I know the type."

"Really?"

"You know the type."

"And?"

"She's not it."

"You can't be sure of that." Adam pushed the possibility out of his head. He'd judged her one way and was not ready to revisit his conclusions, not when seeing her as an innocent opened the door to something almost as dangerous as drugs.

He'd read the file. He knew how deep Knevin was in the meth trade and how close he'd kept Maddie, then Margaret. Knevin ran a huge operation. Employed kids.

It wasn't feasible that she'd stayed ignorant of the guy's activities. Knowing and doing nothing to stop it was arguably as criminal as being actively involved in his dealings.

Zach leaned back with his elbows on the step above him. "You can be so sure of her and her background without having the facts? The media's version of her back then could have been wrong or planted by the prosecution and WitSec."

"Trust me on this."

"If you say so."

"I checked the background." Adam had also contacted the feds on Knevin and even now they were looking for the evidence to file new charges.

"I think you have a problem," Zach said.

"Yeah, what's that?" Adam took a long swig, hating himself for turning to alcohol to hide from the conversation.

"Your usual smooth moves backfire with Maddie."

"I'm not interested in sleeping with her." Now, that was a damn lie. When he wasn't busy saving her, all he thought about was climbing into bed with her. They argued, and he wanted her. She scowled at him, and he wanted her. She was a sickness that had worked her way into his blood and started a fever there.

"Did I mention sex?" Zach smiled when Adam stumbled over his response. "I meant convincing her that she can trust you."

"She can."

"I know that. I also know you're lying because, man, you want to sleep with her."

"I'm not getting sucked in."

Zach clapped Adam on the back. "No offense, but you already are."

"I meant to this conversation."

"I didn't."

Chapter Seven

The door beeped five seconds before it slid open. Luke walked in already in midconversation. "I need help."

Adam sipped his coffee, acting as if seeing his friend handling a weapon and slapping on a Kevlar vest was the most natural sight in the world. "With anything particular or should I start with the list I've been keeping about you?"

"You're funny. Guess that means you got plenty of sleep last night instead of doing something more interesting."

Adam nodded his head. "Nice comeback."

Maddie figured this was a good time to make her presence known. Much more of this and the locker room talk would devolve into something that really ticked her off.

She'd been up for a half hour, staring at the ceiling and wondering what to do about the Adam problem. He hated her for what he thought she'd done in the past. He was clueless on that score, but there was something about him. When he touched her, her nerve endings flared to life. His scent filled her with comfort and his closeness made her smile.

She'd been with a tough guy who commanded attention. She had the broken back and fake identity to prove it. Adam should terrify her. She should flinch and fight to get away from him. The exact opposite was true.

She wanted to chalk up the uncharacteristic lack of control to the frenzied confusion and fear of the past forty-eight hours. Or maybe her hormones had finally sparked to life after being in hibernation post-Knevin.

Either way, she looked at Adam, with his sexy little glasses and killer shoulders, and saw a man who appealed to her on every level.

Luke's voice broke into her useless daydreaming. "I'm looking for surveillance equipment."

"No problem." Adam passed the coffeepot to Zach and took a seat in front of the monitors. "Give me the rundown."

She noticed no one bothered to question Luke or even ask what was with all the firepower. For a second she wondered if this was a chain-of-command thing, then she realized it ran deeper. This was one more example of their unquestioning trust in each other.

"Basically, I need to be able to block tracking and listening devices. Also need a microphone and video feedback to you here, preferably one that can beat someone else's blocking devices." Luke ticked off his list without lifting his head.

"I'm assuming this isn't about Claire," Zach said.

"I'm meeting with Trevor." Luke dropped the gun on the conference table then glanced over at Maddie. "Oh, didn't see you there. Have a good night?"

She glanced at Zach then Adam. "An interesting one."

Adam put a small case in front of Luke. "Repeat the part about seeing Trevor."

"I'm meeting with him."

Adam didn't back down from Luke's no-nonsense tone. "Since when?"

She leaned across the table and whispered to Zach. "Who's Trevor again?"

"Businessman and all-around dirtbag."

"That narrows it down."

Adam broke off his argument with Luke to glance at her. "Bram Walters's brother." He turned back to Luke. "And you're not going alone."

"You'll be in my ear the entire time." Luke lifted the lid to the case and picked up a tiny dot with the tip of his finger.

"Whoever is at the head of this WitSec disaster is getting rid of the extra pieces, the loose ends. We both know Trevor is a player in this game." Adam slid the case out of Luke's reach.

"I'll be fine."

"What makes you think he won't take you out if he gets the chance?"

The conversation kept spiraling. Adam threw out every argument, including Luke's impending fatherhood. She waited for them to roll across the floor throwing fists, but the moment never happened.

Adam could raise his voice without ever lifting an arm in violence. She respected that. Respected him.

She also knew the right answer. "I'm going with Luke."

"You?" Adam's jaw dropped open three times before he spit the word out.

"He won't be expecting me."

"Because he knows we're not stupid enough

to bring you." Adam sliced his arms through the air in an X. "Absolutely not."

"I'm a loose end."

Zach stood up next to Adam. "One we'd like to keep alive."

Adam threw his hands up in the air. "Finally, a reasonable opinion."

"I saw you take down three men in the middle of the dark woods without any help or injuries. I'm betting if there's trouble, then you and Luke can handle one guy in a proper suit in bright daylight. You'll be in public after all, right?"

"You don't understand how dangerous this guy is," Adam said.

"I've been thrown off a building, hunted, shot at and threatened." She counted the horrors on her fingers. "Do you really think I'm afraid of Trevor Walters?"

Adam's voice echoed in the room as he shouted, "That just shows you're not prepared for this."

Silence followed his remark. They all stood around the table, no one moving and Adam's face painted in a mask of fury.

Maddie waited for the usual sensation to hit her. When the world exploded, she tended to pull in and prepare for battle. She could get hit or worse. But she'd lived through the worst and survived. Broken in pieces, maybe, but still breathing.

This time the urge to hide or panic never came. She stepped up and faced Adam down, met him argument for argument. She knew he wouldn't hurt her. She hadn't had that sense of peace or sureness of knowledge since she was a kid.

"The main problem we'd have is that no one can see you. Your cover is in danger already." She could almost hear the wheels turning in Luke's brain as he spoke.

"But we could control the risk," she suggested.

Luke nodded. "True."

"Don't encourage her." Adam spit out the words then stared at Zach as if expecting backup.

She focused on the easiest mark. "Luke, you can sneak me in and out."

"We could cause a diversion with multiple vehicles when you guys leave, make it tough for anyone to follow her," Zach said.

Adam's gaze flipped from Luke to Zach. "No."

She reached across the table and tugged on

Adam's arm to get his attention. "It's not your call."

"I don't know if this is guilt or what." Adam put his free hand over hers. "But you're not sacrificing your life for a discussion with Trevor."

She let the warmth of his skin seep into hers. "I'm trying to get my life back."

"Maddie, no. Not like this."

She blocked out the other men in the room and squeezed Adam's hand. "You'll be there to protect me."

"I still say no." Some of the heat had left his voice.

"But you're so good at rescuing."

THEY REACHED THE RESTAURANT an hour before the scheduled meeting. Luke insisted on getting there first and staking out the place. He'd chosen the spot and set the meeting time right after Trevor's call to prevent him getting set up first.

Adam admired the plan. Luke, as usual, thought out the dangers and limited them. Holden was with the women just in case this meeting was subterfuge, an opportunity for Trevor to launch another attack on Luke's home.

Zach sat in a car a safe distance away,

making sure no one tampered with Adam's truck. And Caleb manned the equipment at the office, even now listening in.

That was all fine. It was the Maddie piece that ticked Adam off. She stood with her feet touching his, wearing Avery's clothes and practically vibrating with excitement. Maddie had no clue how dangerous this assignment was.

It all looked so normal, with Luke sitting at a table in a small private room at the back of the restaurant. The staff and owner weren't there since the place didn't open until dinner. The fact she was hiding behind a curtain, her body flush against Adam's, didn't even faze her.

He didn't know why he cared. Maddie was a grown woman. If she wanted to treat her life like an amusement-park ride, she could. But, damn, the thought of her being hurt—or worse—knocked the breath right out of him.

He admired her spunk and determination. He couldn't imagine living half a life under the constant threat of death and watchful eye of the government. Knowing that piece of crap Knevin sat in a cell somewhere plotting against her made Adam want to jump in the car and issue a threat or two of his own.

"You're pouting." She delivered her assessment standing only a breath away from Adam with her hands pressed against his chest.

The closeness made him twitchy. "Grown men do not pout."

"Do they snarl? Because you are."

He stopped looking over her head and gazed down at her instead. "I don't like this plan."

"You've made that clear."

She rubbed her hand over Adam's chest until he flattened her fingers under his. He doubted she realized she was touching him, let alone caressing him. He knew. His body sure knew.

When this was over...

He couldn't think of that now. "Trevor keeps popping up and every time he does someone dies. I'm trying to make sure it's not you this time," Adam said.

"He called the meeting for a reason."

"Everything he does benefits him. Don't go thinking this is anything other than a calculated maneuver." Adam's gaze went to her mouth, slipped down to her long neck and then back to those lips.

"Then it's good we have one of our own." Her husky voice sucked him in.

"Yeah."

He was going to kiss her. In the middle of a sting with Caleb listening in and Luke a short distance away.

It had been building for days. Weeks, if Adam was honest about it. He'd dreamed about the smoothness of her skin and how amazing it would feel to wrap her toned legs around his waist. Now he would live it.

He lowered his head, giving her plenty of time to pull back. "Be sure."

"I am." She whispered the words against his mouth.

Luke cleared his throat. "He's coming."

Adam jumped, his heart thundering in his ears as he pulled back and realized how close he came to tasting her. Right there at the stake-out. Talk about inappropriate.

Blowing out a long, ragged breath, he balanced his forehead against hers. "Trevor is all yours, Luke."

"Maddie, you only come in if you hear the signal." Luke's low voice carried through the thick velvet curtain separating them.

She couldn't see Luke, but she nodded anyway. "Right."

Adam cupped her cheek before he stepped back and let his hand drop. "Don't worry, boss. I'll keep her here."

"Trevor." Luke didn't get up or extend his hand at the other man's arrival two minutes later.

"Luke." Trevor slid into the seat across from his adversary. "I see you're alone this time. That's unusual. You usually bring men with guns to enforce your point."

"I can handle you."

"If you insist."

Maddie watched the scene unfold on the small screen on Adam's watch. She struggled to listen to the mumbled conversation taking place only a few feet away.

This was the reason she was here, not to climb all over Adam. She repeated that fact several times in her head.

"What do you want?" Luke asked.

Trevor slid an arm across the back of the booth. "No pleasant conversation over the wine list?"

"It's ten-thirty in the morning and we're not friends." Luke's hands stayed under the table.

Maddie knew he held a weapon. So did Adam. Zach could run in with one in only a few seconds.

Trevor glanced around, his gaze stopping on the curtain for a fraction of a second before moving on. "Interesting you picked a new restaurant for our meeting. I preferred our last location."

"Because your listening devices are already in place over there and you have the advantage?"

Trevor held up his hands. "I come in peace, Luke."

"Do tell."

"I have some information you may be interested in."

"Which is?"

Trevor dropped his arms to the table, fixing his jacket sleeves as he did. "It would appear Russell Ambrose was not the top of the WitSec corruption. He collected a lot of money by giving away the locations of the WitSec participants, but he had a boss who grabbed even more."

"Is this a confession?"

"Hardly."

The patronizing grin made Maddie want to reach out and slap the man. Wealth and power oozed off him. She'd seen Trevor on television, giving charitable donations and talking about the good his company did overseas.

She'd never really paid attention to the garbage he spouted, and now she knew it wasn't real. He was corrupt and evil and possibly the reason she was on the run.

"How did you come by this information?" Luke asked.

"You know that has to remain secret. Suffice to say, I have contacts everywhere."

"I'll keep that in mind." Luke sounded bored. "Any idea who the actual head of the kill-for-cash scheme is?"

"Unfortunately, no."

"I thought you might say that." Luke shifted. "Freedom."

"Excuse me?"

At the code word, Adam and Maddie moved out of their hiding place. Adam kept a death grip on her good arm, tucking her to his side. He stood slightly forward. The move put him between her and Trevor. The goal was obvious. He still protected her. That instinct never wavered.

"Trevor." Adam didn't hide his disgust.

"Adam Wright." Trevor's thoughtful expression seemed real, which likely was a testament to his ability to lie on cue. "The glasses are a nice touch. They match your hacker past quite nicely."

"I can beat you to death with or without them on."

"Now I can see why you were so at home hunting in the woods of West Virginia. The sense of lawlessness fits with your blood-thirsty personality."

Maddie caught the reference, the small hint of the past Adam hid, and she tucked it away for later. Now she had to focus on Trevor.

He leaned forward, letting his gaze wander over her. "And who is this?"

Objectively she decided the man was handsome. He had that put-together D.C. look that came with sharp suits and expensive haircuts. She now understood that the perfect facade hid the blood on his hands.

She shifted so he could see her without straining. "I'm the woman you're trying to kill."

"I can tell you have been spending time with the Recovery gentlemen. You share their propensity for exaggeration."

She didn't want to waste one more second in this man's presence. "Call off your henchmen."

"Ma'am, I am not sure what Adam here told you during your time together, but I am a legitimate businessman. I have employees and staff. No henchmen."

He sounded so reasonable, so honest.

She didn't buy it at all. He'd already given hints that he knew about West Virginia.

"What you have is no reason to want me dead."

"I believe that is what I just said."

Adam put his hand on the table and leaned in close to Trevor. "Enough with the games."

Trevor wiggled a finger in the air. "Temper."

"I'll show you just how angry I can get. Call off whichever goon has a weapon trained on me right now and we'll settle this. We'll give it a go. Just you and me."

"You were always the calm one. I wonder what happened." Trevor smiled. "Maybe your lady friend has the answer."

"She's under our protection now," Adam said.

"How charming of you."

"You come after her, we'll view it as coming after us." Luke didn't shout. Just laid it out there in a calm voice.

Trevor made a tsk-tsk sound. "I can hardly be blamed for the danger inherent to a woman in witness protection."

He let the information hang there. She fig-ured it was a deliberate crumb meant to let

Luke and Adam know Trevor was watching everything they did and everyone with whom they came in contact.

Maddie wanted to scream. The man clearly knew who she was and what was happening to her. Yet he pretended to be separate from it all.

"You know our deal," Luke said.

"That covered the Recovery agents only."

"As of this minute she is one. If anyone hurts her—" Luke pointed at Maddie "—we destroy you."

Trevor's blank expression didn't change, but he hesitated before talking again. "I did not realize we were allowed to change the rules in the middle of the game. Maybe I will see fit to make an adjustment of my own."

Adam knocked his fist against the table. "You're allowed to live, to function as a productive member of society even though you should be in jail. That's all you get."

"I am beginning to think this is not a fair exchange."

Adam stood up, lifting his shirt and showing off one of the many weapons he had on him. "Just remember, one step in her direction and it ends for you."

"Clear?" Luke asked.

Trevor gave them a half smile. "It would seem so."

Chapter Eight

Adam looked in the rearview window for the fifth time. The view didn't change. "We have a problem."

"What now?" Maddie turned toward him, but the seat belt held her still. Between the wince and the way she rubbed her lower back, it was clear the pain pills had worn off.

"How long?" he asked.

"What?"

He maneuvered the truck in and out of traffic, but the dark sedan followed. The guy was good. He stayed back, even stopped at a light that Adam blew through on yellow.

If he made the turn after the Air and Space Museum and headed south, Adam would have his answer. At the least he would assume he had a tail and engage in a game of lose-the-jerk.

Adam preferred playing like this only long

after rush hour, when the roads were clearer. He couldn't race through the streets at this time of day. He had to be more subtle, which was not his specialty.

Until he got a handle on the tail situation, he would focus on his other problem. "The pain. How long does it usually last?"

Maddie stared out the window as they waited for the light to turn green. "It's fine."

"But he broke your back."

"It will spasm for a few days and then get back to normal." She traced a finger over the glass. "The pain never stops."

"Maddie…"

"You can go now." She pointed at the green signal.

"Are we done with this topic? We can talk about you being a hacker, if you want. That sounded interesting." She leaned in closer. "Yeah, I heard what Trevor said."

As if Adam needed another reason to punch the guy. In a few short sentences Trevor made it clear he knew a great deal about Adam's past. The time in West Virginia and then the biggie: his life as a hacker-turned-agent.

"The man has an honesty problem."

"So, it wasn't true?" Her bored affect had

disappeared. She was invested in the conversation.

That made one of them. "I mentioned we had a problem. Let's concentrate on that for a second."

She smiled. "What is it?"

He turned left as planned. After two blocks, the sedan followed. "I think we have company."

Her amusement vanished. "We're being followed?"

"Yeah."

She dug her fingernails into his thigh. "By Trevor?"

"I'm thinking by someone he paid."

"We need a diversion. I could—" She stopped when Adam shook his head. "What do you suggest we do?"

"Nothing."

The nails went even deeper. "What kind of plan is that?"

He turned down the radio. They didn't need it since she was screaming over the music. "I expected the tail."

"What about your blocking devices and the special gizmos and all the other stuff…?" She shifted, holding her body stiff and moving only her shoulders as she tried to peek out the side mirror.

When she turned the rearview mirror in her direction, he turned it back. "Stuff?"

"You know. Whatever you call it." She mumbled and fidgeted.

He thought he heard the word *idiot* a few times. "You okay over there?"

"This isn't a game."

She clearly had reached her limit. He covered his tracks every time he drove in or out of Recovery headquarters. He was used to doubling back and driving through restricted areas to throw off potential attackers. He always assumed someone, probably Trevor or his men, was trying to gather intel on Recovery, and Adam acted accordingly. They all did.

He forgot that this wasn't standard for her. "This is how life works. It's what I do."

"And I thought my life was nuts."

"It is right now."

This part of town wasn't as congested as he'd feared, but that left the problem of the street layout. One wrong turn and he'd lose his edge.

"Hang on." He crossed under the Southeast-Southwest Freeway and headed toward the waterfront.

The sedan sped up behind him. The pretense dissolved when the vehicle pulled close enough to fill the rearview mirror. Adam could see the lights and hood and nothing else.

Adam hit a straightaway and gunned it. The truck flew over the holes and divots in the road. Maddie bounced around her seat, wincing with each hard landing, but never complained.

A quick turn sent the truck's back tires spinning. The sound of screeching and the smell of burnt rubber filled the cab. The swift move didn't lose the tail. The sedan hung back for a second, as if suspended in air, then rammed the back of the truck.

Adam's chest slammed into the steering wheel and he grabbed his glasses to keep them from breaking. He would have continued through the windshield except for the seat belt digging into his shoulder.

Maddie braced her arms against the dash, but the force of the hit threw her forward. She covered her head and he struggled to retain control of the vehicle.

"What's the plan now?" She screamed the question from her tucked position. Seemed she was going with panic.

He clicked a button on his watch. "Caleb, we need help."

She grabbed for the handle above the window as the truck's front wheel dipped into a nasty pothole. "Can he get here in time?"

"Caleb can take care of his part from there."

"That's not—"

"Hold tight." Adam slowed down. He saw a few people on the sidewalk and noted their location. The last thing he wanted to do was take out innocent civilians.

"What are you doing?"

"Taking back the advantage."

The sedan edged against the truck's back end. Adam could feel the car bumping and grinding against the metal of his bumper. When the car behind him lurched, Adam hit the brakes and turned his wheel sharp to the right. The truck swerved and bobbed. The sedan smashed into the truck's bed. The hood crumpled under the truck and the driver's hands flew in the air.

Adam smelled gasoline and hot metal but he didn't stick around to exchange insurance cards. He eased on the accelerator, letting the vehicle regain its balance.

Even though they were once again on all

four tires, progress was sluggish. They moved, but the handling was questionable.

So was Maddie. Her shoulders shook from her heavy breathing. "Did you lose him?"

Adam glanced in his rearview mirror. Two men ran toward the sedan but the car stayed still. "We will."

"I don't mean to sound skeptical, but—"

Adam slipped the truck into an alley. When he turned back onto the street at the opposite end, he'd slowed down to compensate for the way the truck's back end kept pulling to the left. "Watch the lights."

"We're in D.C. There's traffic."

"Not as much in this area and not much at all in two seconds." Each light turned green right as they hit the intersection. He didn't even have to tap the brakes.

When the apartment buildings gave way to the industrial area, Adam knew they were going to be fine. He turned off the main road and drove through a series of alleys until they reached a smaller road lined with trucks and work vehicles.

Fifty feet down, a steel gate opened, but not the one to headquarters. This place sat blocks away from Recovery. The only resemblance was the grouping of low-slung warehouses.

Anyone following who didn't know the area would get lost in the maze of buildings.

He slipped into the entrance of the building that purported to deal in medical supplies. Adam knew better. Unless weapons systems for the army were now health related, this place was a front for the military.

As he drove across the parking lot of a building, one gate closed behind them while the one at the opposite end opened. Lots backed up to one another. As he exited one, he'd drive perpendicular across a short street and enter another, creating a makeshift road out of rows of secured parking lots.

Looked as if Caleb had listened during all those sessions in front of the computers. Adam was grateful for the many drills Luke made them perform. They were prepared for just this sort of emergency.

The truck hit a curb and bounced. He was grateful the bumper didn't fall off.

"Be careful of the people." Maddie held her hand out toward the windshield.

Workers stepped out of the way. No one tried to stop them. Adam weaved in and out of the open spaces, going from building to building, mapping out a route where none existed.

He glanced in the mirror and saw only pavement behind him. "It's working."

"Where are the police?"

"Still want to get picked up and rescued by law enforcement?"

"No."

Her answer pleased him more than he wanted to admit. "That's progress."

"Keep your eyes on the road."

He'd rather keep them on her, but she was right. Another look in the mirror confirmed they'd lost their unwanted companion.

He checked in. "Caleb?"

"Gone." The lone word rattled in Adam's ear.

Maddie tugged on his sleeve. "What did Caleb say?"

Adam winked at her and talked to Caleb. "Where is the guy who wanted to play smashup with my truck?"

"He broke away from the crowd of well-meaning citizens. Now he's driving around blind miles away from you."

"The license plate?"

"Wasn't one."

Adam swore. "Figures. Will be there in five."

They continued to drive, circling until the

tires squealed. He guessed they needed air. Looked as if he'd need more than a body shop to put the truck back together again.

He shot her a smile. "We're clear."

"Why, did we finally run out of gas?"

"I meant the chase is over." The rush that came with danger hadn't cooled. It had found a new target: her. "I'm slowing down now because I don't want to attract attention."

"Isn't it a little late for that?"

"Except for the crash on the street, we're fine."

She looked at him, all wide-eyed and spooky, as if he'd lost his mind. "How do you figure that?"

"People tend to see what they want to see. Anyone noticing a truck screaming through a secure lot will think it belongs there. At most they'll complain to management about an out-of-control visitor in the building area."

"What about security? Some of those places had to have cameras poised outside. There were witnesses to the crash."

"Caleb erased all the video evidence by now."

"I thought he was the forensics guy."

"He can press computer keys when I tell him to." They all could.

Every agent could stop bleeding, plant an explosive device and work communications during a job. They had areas of expertise but could back each other up. Another duplication Luke had added to the system when he took over the interim-leadership role that fit him so well.

"And the witnesses on the street?" she asked.

"The plates on the truck won't trace back to me or Recovery…or anyone else."

"When did you set up all this protection?"

"When I installed the system two years ago. I mapped out the entire city, just to be safe. My favorite is the stoplight trick. I've never gotten a ticket and never got caught messing around in District computers. Every time I go in, the metro tech folks spend weeks trying to figure out how the glitch happened."

"You're the glitch."

"Exactly."

She stared at him for a few seconds before talking again. "Are you ever unprepared?"

"I wasn't expecting you." He held her gaze for an extra second before looking ahead again. "Does that count?"

"Meaning?"

They pulled into the Recovery lot. "You figure it out."

TREVOR STALKED INTO his office, brushing past Sela and heading straight for his desk. "Any news?"

She followed behind him and shut the door. When she just stood there, shifting her weight from foot to foot, he knew it was bad. End of the world bad.

His direction had been so simple. He'd used one of his best people. This should have gone off without trouble. But it never worked that way when Recovery was involved.

The biggest mistake Bram ever made was taking away the legitimacy of the group. As a quasi-governmental agency, there was the possibility of oversight and control. As a private organization, they made up their own rules.

Trevor was sick of it.

He stared at Sela. Actually saw her shake. He didn't care. "I am waiting."

"It's not good, I'm afraid."

He sat down nice and slow, letting the rage dissipate as he prepared for the news he knew would ruin his day. "Tell me my guy accomplished something."

"Our signals were blocked, as you suspected they would be."

"Not a surprise."

"We couldn't get a lock on any transmissions or surveillance." She rubbed her hands together as if gathering the strength to keep going. "The restaurant's cameras have been wiped clear, if they were even working in the first place."

"Was he able to tag the vehicles?"

Sela shook her head. "Both Recovery agents checked for devices on the cars. They had someone outside watching over everything."

"Of course they did."

"There was really no way to get the devices on the cars."

Trevor threw his pen down on the desk. It bounced hard enough to travel halfway across the room.

She flinched at his explosion. "I'm sorry."

"Not your fault." He pressed his fingers against his closed eyes and counted to ten before looking up again. "The tail?"

When she visibly swallowed he knew the news wouldn't be good on this front, either. Another round to Luke. The man won entirely too often for Trevor's taste. While he admired the work of the Recovery Project, even Luke's showmanship, the time had come to change the stakes.

Recovery needed to lose a few, but Trevor couldn't allow the responsibility to trace back to him. He also refused to sacrifice his men or risk bringing any more danger into his private life. He had a son and a life to protect. That's why he didn't send his own team in today or do anything to even the odds with Luke.

Trevor needed a target and someone to take the potential fall. John Tate was perfect for both.

"Well?" Trevor asked the question in the most reasonable voice he could muster.

Sela didn't deserve his wrath and he couldn't afford to lose her. From the way she cowered, her shoulders folded in on her, she wasn't taking his show of temper well now.

He rarely lost his cool around her. Not that he showed that side to anyone. Not anymore. He'd learned that lesson from Russell and that tape.

"Our guy lost Adam's car," she said.

"Where?"

"Southwest."

"Okay." He struggled to regain the rest of his smooth control. He could handle this the way he handled everything else. The blackmail, Bram's death, the loss of good men to

Recovery. It all rolled over him. "I'll find another way."

"Is there anything I can do?"

"No." He had to figure this part out on his own.

Chapter Nine

Maddie stumbled through Recovery headquarters' door ready to sit down and put her feet up. Confused feelings about Adam and pure exhaustion pulled at her. The wild ride through the city didn't help, either.

"Here she is."

Luke's voice registered, as did Adam's hand against her back. All she wanted was a handful of painkillers and a moment of quiet. Looked as if she wasn't going to get either.

Adam's fingers clenched against her shirt. "Vince? What are you doing here?"

She raised her head and saw one of the men who'd ushered her into a new life in witness protection. His presence struck her as out of place in the middle of the industrial surroundings. She remembered Zach's suggestion that they not involve Vince Ritter in their plans and woke right up.

Zach sat at the conference table now, watching Vince's every move. The stiffening of Adam behind her mirrored the tension she saw in Zach's face. Luke stood with his usual unreadable expression.

"I wanted to check in and see if you had any news on Rod." Vince shook Adam's hand, then looked at her. "Maddie?"

"It's good to see you, Vince."

The man hadn't changed much over the years. He was in his late fifties, with graying hair and sharp green eyes. He always looked more suited to a tennis court, with a sophisticated yet athletic air about him.

She knew he'd retired early, as soon as the government retirement system allowed. She had no idea what he did now because she wasn't permitted to have contact with him once he ceased being her handler. During the time they'd worked together, she'd lived in Florida. Her transfer to West Virginia had come after that. Vince hadn't had access to her records then and shouldn't have known her whereabouts.

Rod had somehow known, though. He lived near West Virginia and had wandered into her diner one day. She'd never figured out if it was an accident or an informal check-in. They'd acted like strangers, but knowing he was close had made her feel safe.

Those days were gone.

"Did you know I was here?" she asked.

Vince looked around the room. "Funny, but Luke didn't share that. No one did."

Luke shrugged. "It's new information."

"And top secret, of course. No one but us knows she's here." Adam's comment sounded more like a warning.

He left unspoken the warning that if anyone came looking for her, he'd blame Vince. But Maddie heard it. She'd spent enough time with him to know when he was issuing a challenge.

Vince rocked back on his heels with his hands in his pockets. "What about Trevor? He must be looking for her."

"I said no one knows," Adam replied. "Only the people in this room know her whereabouts."

"It goes without saying I'll stay quiet." Vince smiled in her direction. "I'm surprised you weren't relocated after the Russell Ambrose corruption came to light. Your WitSec cover is likely blown."

The face she used to find kind now raised a red flag in her head. She crowded closer to

Adam, absorbing his heat and trying to send a silent signal.

Between the anxiety bouncing around her stomach and her sore back, she could barely stand. It was a relief when Adam leaned in and held her up.

"We decided she was safer with us," he said.

Vince laughed. "Than with the entire Marshals Service?"

No one joined in his amusement, least of all Adam. "Yeah."

Vince held Adam's gaze. The tense silence dragged on as he looked from face to face without saying a word.

She thought about breaking the heavy mood before they all drowned in it. The longer they stood, the taller and bigger the Recovery team looked. She knew it was an optical illusion or a trick played by her malfunctioning brain. She felt the air being squeezed out of the room.

"Now that I think about it, that's probably about right." Vince's chest rose and fell on a heavy exhale. "You guys can handle it."

Luke crashed through the rest of the unspoken hostility with one clap of his hands. The sharp thwack set the room in motion again. "Okay, then."

Vince's shoulders relaxed. "Right. What about Rod?"

"We don't have news," Luke said as he offered Vince a soda.

The older man waved it off. "I was afraid of that."

"He's in hiding. He'll pop up."

Luke didn't say goodbye, but Maddie heard the finality in his words. He wanted Vince out. The not-so-subtle message was that Vince should call first from now on.

"I hope so." Vince glanced at the door. "Well, if there's nothing for me to review, I guess I'll be going."

"We'll keep you informed." Luke shook the other man's hand while guiding him toward the door.

Vince waved over his shoulder. "Maddie, stay safe. Remember the rules and your training."

"Always."

She heard the steel door slam shut as she looked at the faces of the men in the room. They all looked so serious, and for the first time she could remember, they were quiet. No one joked or talked.

"I got it." Adam slipped into the tech seat and watched Vince's car leave the fenced-in lot outside. After a few keystrokes he leaned back. "Codes are changed."

Zach groaned. "I just memorized the last set."

"You'll memorize these, too." Luke walked back into the kitchen and grabbed a glass. "They change often enough for this to be routine by now."

It was as if they wanted to be normal and didn't know how. The grumbling and stomping around would have been comical if it didn't center around a possible conspiracy and a series of murders.

She waited until Zach, Luke and Adam sat down at the table before she asked, "What was that about? I asked before about Vince and you pretended everything was fine. Now, talk."

Adam's head shot up. "I don't know—"

"Oh, please. You guys almost kicked Vince out of here."

"We said goodbye," Caleb joked.

"I thought he was one of you."

Zach snorted. "Definitely not."

Adam didn't try to hide his anger. He shifted around in his seat like a little boy on a time-out. "I don't like Vince showing up right now, without any warning or an invitation.

And while you just happen to be here. It's too convenient."

Since Vince was there when they got back, she figured he was in on the Trevor sting. Thinking he just happened to be there at that time sent a twist of dread through her.

She no longer believed in avoiding questions. She'd once lived her life without questioning the facts, blindly accepting that the income that appeared on a daily basis was clean and that the men in and out of her apartment were her boyfriend's real friends. She didn't have Adam's brains, but she did learn a lesson when it got drummed in her head by a prosecutor who was more than willing to hang the blame around her neck and throw her in jail.

"Did Vince have the codes for the building?" she asked.

"I let him in." Everyone zoned in on Caleb as he spoke. "I made sure you were all safe first, of course. But when Vince showed up I thought it was odd and I wanted to see what he wanted."

"Which was?" Adam asked.

Caleb's eyebrow lifted. "Nothing he couldn't have asked over the phone."

Apparently no one trusted Vince.

"You guys think he's involved in this WitSec thing," she said.

"It's not clear." Luke held up a hand when Adam tried to butt in. "We hope not, but Vince has inside information on WitSec and the two women who are now dead because someone paid for their information. He has details about you, and you were almost killed, too. It seems like a pattern."

"So does Rod." She regretted the comment when Adam flinched.

Luke took it in stride. "True, but we worked with Rod. He formed this team. Vince has always been an outside guy. Even Rod didn't bring Vince in as a Recovery partner, which says something."

This time Adam smiled when he lifted his head and looked around the table. "No wonder she thinks we're paranoid."

"Wrong." She had their attention now. "I think you're smart."

IT TOOK ALL AFTERNOON and hours of talking through the possible scenarios of what Vince knew and when before the warehouse quieted down. Luke and Caleb went back home to their wives. Holden signed off on the video feed. Even Zach made himself scarce, but not before announcing he wouldn't be back until morning.

That left Adam alone with Maddie. He went from assured and wound up over having to see Trevor in person to unsure of his moves.

She was injured and on the run. She'd been through so much and dragged around more baggage than even he could carry.

Yet, he wanted her.

He settled for standing there with a stupid grin on his face while she gathered the blankets and sheets for him to sleep on the couch downstairs. She paraded around in a short pajama outfit that Avery and Caleb dropped by.

The outfit was innocent enough, consisting of short shorts and a V-neck sleeveless top. It would have been fine if it didn't highlight her legs every time she bent over the bed or show off her flat stomach when she lifted her arms even a little bit.

The flimsy outfit was killing Adam. If he didn't know better, he'd say Avery sent it on purpose to drive him slowly insane with need.

"You did a good job tonight." He fumbled the words like a preteen on his first date.

"You mean when I was playing along and keeping information from Vince?"

He nodded. "You're getting good at that."

"Disobeying WitSec protocol?" Maddie dropped the stack of linens on the edge of the bed and stood in front of him. "Yeah, thanks."

He gave in to the need to touch her and ran his hand up and down her bare arm. "How are you feeling?"

"Like I'm put together with Silly String."

That killed the building mood.

He dropped his arms. "I should let you rest."

He got to the edge of the steps before she started talking. Her usually firm voice stumbled as she spoke.

"Knevin figured out I was talking to the prosecutor. That's why he did it."

Adam turned to face her but didn't say a word. Not now when she'd finally opened up.

"I thought I'd been so clever, sneaking around and reporting back. I never went to a lawyer's office. The information exchange happened in the open to hide what we were really doing."

Adam leaned against the railing, not moving closer for fear of startling her or making her stop talking.

Her hands stayed at her sides as her gaze centered on his chest. "But Knevin figured it out. He had an informant in the police department. Someone tipped him off."

"Figures." Adam hoped that guy was in jail, too.

"I was so impressed with doing the right thing, I didn't pick up on the clues until I was on the roof and he was lifting me into the air."

The flat way she described the horror shook him. Actually rattled his bones so hard he was surprised she didn't hear the clanking. "You survived."

"Because I wasn't the only one on the inside. Someone in the organization who happened to work for the feds and was planted inside got word to the police, and medical attention came right away. It was the difference between me breathing out of a machine forever and living a somewhat normal life, if you can call this that."

"I can't believe Knevin didn't try again. Until now, I mean."

Her big eyes filled with sadness. "He thought I was dead, was told I was. He even identified my body, but through a glass so he couldn't see me breathing."

She hadn't just played dead, she'd almost been dead. "I'm sorry."

"I went into the program, came out for the trial and went back in again."

Adam knew the parts she didn't say. The file he had on her covered this part of her life. She'd lost her mother after she'd given up her natural right to publicly grieve. She went from a community-college dropout working an administrative-assistant job in a high-rise office building to running a diner in a small town.

Her cooking skills were self-taught. Based on the fact he'd gained four pounds since eating her food, she was pretty good at it.

"I never dealt drugs." She came to him and skimmed her fingertips across his shoulders, burning a line of fire with her touch.

"We don't have to talk about this."

"I know you don't believe me, but I need you to hear me say the words." He'd reread her file that morning while she slept. The police and prosecutor on her case all believed she was an active participant. The notes indicated an admission.

Still, he couldn't see it. He remembered Zach's adamant denial of the idea. Adam's head said her past should disgust him. The rest of him found her innocent.

He wrapped his arms around her, letting his hands fall loose near her lower back for fear of injuring her further. "Why do you care what I think?"

She frowned. "Do you really not know?"

So the attraction went both ways. The energy pulsing around them zinged through the room. Being this near to her only made him want to pull her in closer.

The more he learned, the more he wanted. "Lie down."

Her hand swept across his jaw. "That's a pretty big change in conversation. Kind of bold."

He planned to get there, but he wanted to earn it. "You were limping. I'm going to massage your leg."

She tried to pull back, but he held her still. "That's not a great idea, Adam. I've had all sorts of physical therapy. The cure is as bad as the pain."

"Trust me."

"You ask a lot."

"Get on the bed."

She hesitated, then slowly slipped out of his grasp and walked to the side of the bed. She didn't climb onto the mattress or invite him any closer.

He would have to take the lead. "Let me."

He followed her. With a hand on her elbow,

and as gently as possible, he helped her turn around. When she just sat there, he coaxed her into lying diagonally across the comforter.

She fought even that much. She half sat and half lounged. "I'm not sure about this."

"I can see that."

When he kneeled on the bed next to her, she let her upper body fall against the mattress. The position left her open to his touch. Those long, lean legs stretched out from under her shorts and went on forever. He saw creamy skin and the results of her long runs through the woods.

With a light touch, he ran his hands up her legs. The smooth flesh sent his body into overdrive. Gone were thoughts of protection and being reasonable. He wanted to be inside her.

Instead, he concentrated on working the tightness out of her muscles. Over and over he kneaded her legs, working with careful strokes to smooth out the knots. He lost track of time as he poured all his healing energy into her.

An erection pushed against his jeans and his brain scrambled with fantasies of what he wanted to do to her, but he limited the touching to massage. As he smoothed his way to the juncture between her legs and butt, he looked his fill and couldn't prevent a stray caress.

When she groaned, his hands stilled and he lifted them from her legs.

"Adam?"

"Yeah?" He couldn't lower his hands to her skin again. If he did, they'd snake under her shorts and the moment would shift from comfort to sex.

With his help, she turned over, lying on her back with her hands over her head. From this position he could see the sliver of bare, sexy stomach peeking beneath her shirt. The only thought in his mind was about how much he wanted to taste her.

He was a goner.

"I'm trying to be decent here."

"Why?" She slipped her hand down his side to land on his outer thigh.

"I don't want to hurt you." He hoped like hell she didn't ask if he meant physically or emotionally, because he didn't know anymore.

"I'm a grown woman."

"Definitely. Grown and rounded in all the right places."

"I take responsibility for my actions."

He shut that one out because he knew she was talking about more than sex. "But your back…"

"You'll be gentle."

When she held out an arm to him it was like lighting the welcome sign. He gave in. He lowered his body over hers, careful to balance his weight on his elbows.

She slipped his glasses off. He could still see her just fine.

His mouth dipped, taking her lips against his in a shattering kiss. His hands cradled her face. Her fingers dived into his hair. He wondered how he had gone this long without the sensation of her mouth against his.

Before he could pull back and think through all the cons, he let his fingers wander. He brushed his hand over her breast, cupping and caressing. When his mouth followed, even through the thin cotton, her shoulders lifted off the bed.

It was all the encouragement he needed.

He stripped her shorts and panties down her legs. Sitting up on his knees, he pulled his T-shirt out of his jeans as his gaze toured her toned body. She joined in, peeling the shirt up and over his head.

Then he was kissing her again. He wanted the contact of skin on skin. Separating their bodies only long enough to drag her shirt off, he threw the garment on the floor and came back down on top of her.

"Am I hurting you?" He asked the question while treating her to a line of kisses down her neck.

Another few inches and the tip of her breast was in his mouth and her hands were on his belt. His fingers went to his pocket. He dug around for the condom and dropped it on the mattress next to her head.

It was a frenzy of rough breathing and rolling bodies. He protected her back with his hands as his mouth learned her taste. His fingers and tongue traveled over her until she begged him to end it.

He let go of her only long enough to open the condom. The tearing noise echoed through the dark room but didn't stop them.

Her hands found him as he fumbled to get the condom on. When her hips bucked under him and she whispered his name, he lost the last of his control.

He settled between her legs and dipped his finger inside her one last time. She was wet and ready. The pink flush of her cheeks and the eager roaming of her hands ended the sensual foreplay.

With one long stroke he pushed into her. Her body clung to him inside and out. He cradled her back, trying to ease the pressure on her as he slid in deeper. His body begged to perform a steady rhythm, but she needed a calmer meeting.

Slow and steady he pressed in and pulled out until the pressure built and she tightened around him. When he touched his finger against her, her head flew back and her body trembled in his arms.

Her pleasure touched off his. In the heated sheets, with sweat beading on his forehead and his muscles shaking from the force of his orgasm, he let go. His body clenched and unleashed.

The darkness enveloped them as they moved and moaned. Satisfaction came hard and fast, leaving them both out of breath. When he rolled off her he held her hand, afraid to break the contact.

His other arm draped over his eyes. "Wow."

She kissed the back of his hand then rested their joined palms back on her breast. "I'm happy I ignored protocol and never made that call."

He smiled in the darkness. "Me, too."

"I figured now might be a good time to tell you something."

Here it was. He readied his mind for the blow to come. He suspected the truth about the drugs, but hearing her admit the truth after all those other lies would cost him something. "Go ahead."

She dragged their hands up her body until the back of his touched her cheek. "I met with Rod a few months ago. It's possible I was the last one to see him before he disappeared."

Chapter Ten

John Tate fiddled with the penholder at the edge of Trevor's desk. "You didn't tell me you planned to meet with Luke."

"I did not realize I was answerable to you." Trevor walked to the floor-to-ceiling window behind his desk. He didn't sit down, didn't offer John a chair.

"Well, you are."

As far as Trevor was concerned, the era of John dropping by was over. This would be their last six-o'clock meeting before the office buzzed with life.

"I think we need to have a discussion about our arrangement." And if John failed to back down, Trevor would shove him down.

"It's simple. You made plans to have your wife murdered, I found out and now I own you."

The comment used to cut through Trevor,

reminding him of a single moment of stunning intellectual lapse. One point in time that haunted him and tainted every move thereafter.

But as John repeated the refrain, the sting lessened. Trevor knew the release of the tape would guarantee his ruin and likely cost him his son. He also realized following the lead of the idiot in front of him could do the same.

"What do you think this information buys you?" Trevor asked.

"Cooperation."

That had not been the case so far, so Trevor marveled that John could think it would be true now. "And?"

"Whatever else I decide I need."

"You are playing a dangerous game."

John lifted a gold pen from Trevor's collection and put it in his pocket. "And I'm winning."

"How did we decide that exactly?"

"I found the one piece of information you couldn't."

But John conveniently ignored the demons nipping at his heels. Trevor knew John had turned from legitimate government employment to a murder conspiracy for a reason.

Trevor vowed to find it.

"Go ahead. I am listening."

"The location of Recovery headquarters. I know what's in the building, the equipment they have, even the security codes to get in."

It took all Trevor's energy and willpower not to show a reaction. "You are a government talking head. How did you gain access to those particulars?"

"I have friends." John turned the photo on the edge of the desk and stared at it.

"I somehow doubt that." The thought of John interacting with his son, even through a picture, made Trevor homicidal.

The killing rage bubbled up inside him to the point of overflowing. He was ten seconds away from making another irreversible mistake.

"I do wonder that if I can get information on my own and if I have my own men at my disposal, why do I need you?"

Something clicked inside Trevor. The pieces fell together in his mind until he wondered how he'd missed the obvious before. "You have a partner."

John froze. "What?"

"Someone on the inside of Recovery, though I cannot imagine Luke failing to ferret out a mole." Trevor ran through the team roster in his head. "Possibly Zach. That spooky quiet could hide something deeper. The others, no."

But it all made sense. John might act as if he ran the operation but he was just a player. He probably did not possess one sip more power than Russell Ambrose had.

It never fit that John would have access to men who would kill for him. He wielded a great deal of power, but it was legitimate power with oversight and political restraints. He rose through the government system and caught the attention of the right people in the party. But he was a suit, not a visionary or even a leader.

John placed the photo back on the desk face-down. "I told you I knew people."

"I could never see you interviewing the criminal element, lowering yourself to meet with the type of people who get paid to perform dirty jobs and who work without the restraints of loyalty."

"My resources are endless."

Trevor still had to unravel the biggest secret. That would take time unless John slipped up. "I would say your partner is not one of the Recovery team. Not an active member. Probably someone tangential."

John waved him off. "You don't need to

worry about who you work for. You just need to do what we tell you."

Now that Trevor knew he was dealing with someone other than John, the man's significance decreased to zero. Trevor needed the name. The real leader.

He tried out a theory. Rolled it around in his brain to see if it passed the logic test. "Maybe Rod changed sides, got tired of playing by the rules and earning a pittance of a salary."

"I didn't say that."

"You two were whining over dinner one evening and hatched a grand scheme to collect money and get rid of the evidence?"

John's smirk disappeared. "We're not talking about—"

Power poured through Trevor. He felt the old confidence return, fueling his every thought and move.

Now he had a direction.

"I assume that's what happened. You got tired of seeing your friend's success and wealth and decided to get your share the easiest way possible." Trevor could not hide his amusement and did not try. "Why work when you can steal, right, John?"

"That's enough."

Trevor pulled out his chair and sank into it.

"I want to meet your partner. I need to know exactly who I am dealing with before we go one step further."

"That's never going to happen."

And now he knew he was right.

John had slipped and provided the one nugget Trevor had not found on his own: confirmation. Once Rod, or whoever really ran the show while letting John think he did, understood the stakes and the liability John presented, John would be gone. Until then, Trevor would tolerate John Tate. Use him.

Trevor cleared his throat to cover his smug satisfaction. "Then you tell me what you think *is* going to happen."

"The assignment has not changed. You will destroy Recovery. Take them all out, including their women."

"That is very chivalrous of you."

John started to move around. His hands and feet were in constant motion. "I know the role Mia played in your brother's death. I'd think that would give you sufficient reason to take her out. And Avery helped bring down Russell. They are just as much of a problem as the men."

Trevor decided to play along. It would not hurt to let John think he was about to get his way. Might even bring this scenario one step closer to the real power center, whether that was Rod or one of the Recovery team.

"Ah, I see. This is your brilliant gas-leak idea."

"You have two days."

That amounted to the one threat too many. Trevor now had a timeline—not for the battle John wanted, but for one much bigger. "Or?"

"I will follow my partner's advice and remove you from the equation."

There was no question about it now. John was not in charge. He likely held as little power as Russell had. Since no one had come calling after Russell's funeral, Trevor realized the man had not been essential to the operation except for his handler contacts.

"Do you understand where you are or the firepower I have at my disposal right at this minute? What I could do to you if I chose?" Trevor asked the questions in a soft voice despite his fury.

"My tape trumps your gunmen."

The man had obviously never been shot. Trevor was thrilled he would be the one to correct that oversight. "We may not agree on that point."

"You've been warned. Two days then I visit your ex-wife's attorney."

Instead of fighting off a new round of panic, Trevor started the mental countdown to John's destruction.

Chapter Eleven

Adam lectured her during the entire drive from D.C. to western Maryland. When they finally pulled into the long dirt driveway leading to Rod's farm, Maddie was relieved she'd soon have the opportunity to get out of the confined space.

Adam kept up the constant stream of talk even as he disarmed Rod's alarm and opened the gated entrance to the property. When he parked, she almost shot out of the car. Anything to escape the drone of Adam's voice as he made his disappointment clear. In twelve hours he'd managed to turn from sexy bed partner to this.

She slammed the door to the truck Adam borrowed from somewhere, she didn't know where and didn't bother to ask, and jumped down to the gravel.

He followed her.

"Are you done?" She looked past the parallel lines of tall bending trees to the two-story stone house at the back of the property.

"What?"

"Yelling."

"I'm trying to have a discussion."

"With yourself, apparently, because you don't seem interested in my side."

He slapped an open hand against the truck, staring at the paint instead of her. "We were together for three days."

"More than—" She stopped when his head flew up and he pinned her with a look of green-eyed fury.

"At no point did you think it would be a good idea to mention your recent contacts with Rod?"

"Not recent."

"Maddie."

"No, I didn't."

"I'm wondering why."

It all came down to trust, but it was hard to explain that to a man who'd spent the entire night before making love to her and the past two hours going out of his way to wipe the good memories from her mind.

"We didn't exactly start out on a share-and-share-alike basis, Adam."

"Maybe when we were in West Virginia and that first night on the run, but surely after that."

"Rod was once my handler. I never expected him to walk back into my life." She knew they stood on acres of private land, but she glanced around and lowered her voice just in case. "We didn't discuss my case or anything personal. I served him dinner at the diner and he left."

"You didn't think it was a little odd that the guy who'd watched over you in Florida turned up living just a few miles away from your address in West Virginia?"

"Not then."

"When, Maddie?"

"When I sat in that warehouse and listened to you guys tell me about the women in the WitSec program who were murdered for cash and about your missing boss." The cool air rushed through her hair, chilling her skin through her borrowed long-sleeve shirt.

"That was still two days ago."

"I guess it slipped my mind to unload every last detail of my usually boring life, what with being chased and shot at and all."

Adam's shoulders fell as if all the steam had rushed out of him, leaving the nice Adam behind. "I see."

She couldn't believe that was all he had to say. "What?"

He pushed away from the truck and walked toward her. His black T-shirt stretched across his chest. Tall, with muscles everywhere she looked, he overwhelmed her. His massive body shut out the bright sunshine, and even the birds stayed quiet while he stalked toward her.

"Fine." The word sat out there, delivered through a half smile with a dimple that mesmerized her.

Seeing him close stole her breath. Not out of fear. Out of the knowledge of what he could do with that mouth and those hands. Because of the solid man he turned out to be behind those thin wire-framed glasses.

"I still don't know what you're saying." The comment sounded breathy even to her ears.

He drew two fingers down a strand of hair to where it curled at the end. "Exactly what I said. We're fine."

She shot him her best you've-lost-your-mind look, which was tough, since all she wanted to do was drag him back to headquarters and the bed waiting upstairs.

No one except Zach knew they were gone. It was possible that by now he had filled in the team about the unplanned trip and was on the way to provide backup.

"Good," she said, because she didn't know what else to say.

When he didn't respond except to put his hand on the small of her back and guide her down the path toward the house, she realized it was that easy for him. He blew his cool, stated his case and then moved on. The anger didn't fester until it exploded in violence. He would never raise a hand to her or cause her pain.

Well, not physically. But he had the ultimate power to destroy her in other ways. She'd given him that by letting him become important.

For a woman who'd spent years avoiding any attachment that could be ripped away from her, it was a terrifying step. As scary as waking up in a hospital to men in suits and a tube down her throat.

"I'm assuming you've searched Rod's house before," she said.

"Yep." Adam's watchful gaze never stopped moving. He looked from side to side with his weapon drawn.

There were a million places for someone to hide. A shed near the front of the property, thick trees and the sides of the house she couldn't see. Then there was the entire area to her right, which was flush with vegetation so thick she couldn't tell what lingered on the other side. The left gave way to an orchard of shorter trees just starting to fill in. Anyone could be inside the grove.

The entire detour to this part of Maryland struck her as dangerous. Even if Zach was manning the surveillance of the place and watching them from miles away, he couldn't get to them in time.

The sudden side trip here intrigued her. "So, why the big rush to get me here?"

"You know your past and the way WitSec operates. You might see something in the house we missed. A clue that could explain where Rod is since nothing else has."

"I doubt it."

"We might not know it's important without you pointing it out."

She stopped on the bottom step of the front porch. "I get it."

Adam stopped, too. "Care to fill me in?"

"You think Rod arranged for me to be moved closer to him."

Adam accompanied his quick glance to the side with a whispered profanity. "Are you always so quick to pick up on stuff?"

"Next time kidnap a dumb chick."

He nodded, smiling as he did. "Yeah, it's possible."

"But Rod didn't have access to my file."

"He clearly did or I wouldn't have the information I have. It wasn't complete, but it was enough to start tracking you. My whole goal was to get to you before the person who paid for your information could."

"But the idea of Rod shifting my life around from outside WitSec? I don't know how he'd have access or a say." With all the secrecy surrounding witness protection, the option didn't strike her as realistic.

"I have no idea. It's not as if I understand Rod or his choices lately. All I can tell you is that the man I knew before the walls closed in and he took off had a plan for everything." Adam ushered her up the steps and then turned around to survey the acres of land they'd just covered by car and foot.

He clicked a button on his watch. With one last look, he seemed to focus on something on the lawn that she couldn't detect. Finally satisfied, he stepped up to the front door and flipped down the small panel to the left.

A hand scanner. She stared at it and then at Adam. "Are you kidding?"

"It's some of my finest work." He actually sounded offended as he said it.

"Is anywhere safe for you guys without all the bells and whistles of technology?"

"I think I've mentioned our preference to be prepared." He fit his hand against the blue panel. The door clicked a second later.

"What did you do a second ago with your watch?"

"I reactivated the sensors. Someone steps in the wrong place around here, I'll know." He walked her inside.

"Computer geek."

"Insurance." He breathed the word against her hair.

"Don't be offended. I think you're a very sexy computer geek."

"Nice."

The smell hit her first. She expected a musty, closed-up assault on her senses akin to the mothball scent of her grandmother's attic. But she sniffed and picked up notes of pine and bleach.

"Did someone just clean the place?"

"We did. We ripped it apart, moved stuff around, generally made a mess and then tried to clean up in case Rod did come back." Adam typed a series of numbers into the pad on the inside of the door.

The truth smacked her. "You don't think he will."

"We should start downstairs."

"Adam, answer me."

His shoulders, so broad and proud, slumped. "No. Not anymore. Rod would be with us if he wanted to and if he were able."

Her heart ached for Adam, for the look of defeat around the corner of his mouth and the pain she heard in his voice. At least she knew what she was giving up when she made her choice. She'd walked away.

At the moment she didn't even have a piece of underwear to her name. She ran out of West Virginia leaving everything, including the emergency bag, behind. But she wasn't the one who was abandoned.

Adam didn't have that luxury. Someone he respected and cared about took off without a word. For the first time she felt the other side of the guilt. The unending sadness and paralyzing anger of not knowing.

"Let's start in the office." Adam's running shoes squeaked against the hardwood as he opened the pocket door to the nearest room.

Judging by the big desk and walls of books,

this was the office. Probably the place where Rod worked as the rest of the team checked in by computer.

In silent agreement, they went to work. They'd shuffled papers and checked every drawer for a half hour before she realized something was off. Adam turned over folders and paged through books but he wasn't concentrating. Wasn't even keeping watch at the window for attackers the way he usually did.

The man was always on, his instincts aware and alive to the point where they crackled. Now he kept a close guard on his watch, but that was it.

She threw the binder on Rod's desk, letting it slap against the metal top. "Okay, tell me."

Adam broke off his love affair with his watch. "What?"

"Why are we really here?"

"I told you."

His expression never changed, but she heard the lie. Maybe it was the intimacy of the night before that clued her in, but the thread of dishonesty was clear. He was hiding something and failing at it.

"You wouldn't risk taking me out in public

without a good reason." She'd been with him nonstop for days and knew how he operated.

He kept her closed off in a place he controlled. All the Recovery men handled their women that way. A joyride outside the metro area violated all the rules.

Adam tilted his head to the side and showed off that dimple. "We're collecting evidence."

She wasn't buying it. "We're pushing stuff around and wasting time."

"Maybe you should leave the investigation to the professionals."

"Coming here to take a brief look around is nonsense." She pointed at him. "You shut off the phones while you sleep and hover while I use the bathroom."

"I think you're exaggerating."

"Then let me call Luke." She held out her hand and wiggled her fingers at him. "Give me your cell."

Adam blew out a long breath as he placed his hand in hers. "I thought I could get away with it."

She tried to tug away from him but he held on tight. "What?"

"It's for your protection."

"You say that a lot. What does it mean in this context?"

Adam leaned against the desk with his legs open and her body tucked between them. "Luke believes someone was going to breach the warehouse to get to you."

Her thoughts scrambled. "We have to get back there. They might need us."

"We're staying here until it's clear."

HOLDEN TAPPED HIS PEN against his front teeth. "Any chance Adam was wrong?"

Luke scoffed. "Is he ever?"

"I refuse to answer that on the grounds he might have a listening device in here and would never let me forget the compliment."

"He said someone tried to hack into the system last night. That means someone knew where to look." Luke leaned over Caleb's back and watched the monitors protecting the warehouse and the others at his house.

The women were on the couches under the stairs trading thoughts on Maddie and how long it would be before Adam came to his senses. Zach was on the road to Adam. The team had fanned out, but they all had weapons and were hunkered down in buildings with top security.

The breach could come from any direction. Spreading out to cover every option was the right answer, but having Adam so far away made the nerve at the back of Luke's neck throb. The only mistake was in not sending Zach as immediate backup at Rod's place.

"You think the cyberattack was orchestrated by Trevor?" Caleb said more to the room at large than to any person in particular.

Luke glanced through the file in front of him again, looking for any bit they may have missed. "Most likely."

Holden lowered his arm as he dropped the pen. "What does that mean for the peace deal we allegedly have with this dirtbag?"

Luke didn't have to weigh the pros and cons on that one. The answer was automatic. "It's over. We can attack at will, as far as I'm concerned."

Caleb grunted. "It's about damn time."

"I just want him to give me the excuse to remove him for good." Luke could take the heat, but this would be a raging fire. He wanted to be ready.

Only way they'd survive without prison time was to have a reason to take Trevor out. Luke thought they had it. He just needed the right evidence to convince the right powerful person, then the deed would stay quiet and private. Trevor would be just another businessman who suffered a fall. Hell, he could claim early retirement for all Luke cared. The important thing was to remove Trevor from power.

"Maybe we can finally take care of this tonight," Holden said.

"Maybe." But Luke's instincts told him something was seriously wrong.

Chapter Twelve

Maddie accepted the news better than Adam expected. She didn't yell or argue. She frowned at him and walked out of Rod's den. Adam waited a few minutes before following. The check-in with Luke still shook him. All was quiet on that end. That should have been good news, but it made Adam jumpy.

Hacking followed by a lack of movement didn't make sense. Trevor—someone—should be pushing in by now. The person who'd attacked the system didn't get in, but they'd tried. Alarms had shrieked before four that morning and prevented the worst from happening, but not before the hacker got led on a chase to nowhere.

The person didn't leave footprints that took them anywhere helpful, but it was clear someone was obsessed with tracking them all down. The inevitable rush to safety for Maddie was his idea, but Luke agreed. He wanted to spread the team out and make the fight against them as difficult as possible.

Adam walked through the dining room and into the country kitchen beyond. The usual creaks of an old house accompanied him. There was no sign of Maddie inside, but the back door was open. Just past the small paved patio he caught a glimpse of her hair. Standing by the sink, he watched her out the window, seeing her pick a leaf and twirl it between her hands.

Since they'd been there, the wind had kicked up and the sun had begun to slide down the horizon. Her hair flipped around in the breeze, with the light catching and highlighting the deep auburn strands. She was beautiful, with a swimsuit model's body and a brain that left him breathless just trying to keep up.

He'd dated often since losing Robyn to another man's bottle of vodka. He enjoyed the temporary satisfaction that came with moving from conversation to the bedroom, no matter how many hours or days it took. He hadn't wanted anything more. Not for years.

That was before he met Maddie.

They had a few hours before darkness, and then he'd have to make a decision. The idea of a repeat performance of last night shot life into the lower half of his body and pushed out the worries for his team. But his lower half had never been good at critical thinking. As he watched her now in her slim dark jeans, a war waged inside him. He no longer knew which side he wanted to win.

When she passed the line of trees to investigate the covered pool behind, he decided to call a halt to her sightseeing. Roaming around was a dangerous game.

As he opened the screen door to retrieve her, his watch chirped. He glanced at the small monitor then back to Maddie. She'd slipped to the opposite side of the pool and well out of range for him to grab her and go.

He threw the door open as the buzzing on his watch turned to a steady alarm. That meant one thing: penetration.

"Maddie!"

She lifted her head, her smile fading as he broke into a run. The leaf twirled to the ground and her eyes narrowed with confusion.

"Come here!"

She started toward him as the figures appeared over the hill behind her.

"Get down!" He shouted the command as he dropped to his knees.

Hands up and steady, he fired, picking off the one in the best position to get off a shot first. The guy moved forward, though hit in the shoulder. Adam didn't make the same mistake twice. His second shot smashed into the guy's forehead and took him down.

Shots rang out through the quiet countryside. He dived behind the patio table. Glass shattered as the windows behind him exploded in a rain of bullets. Shards blanketed him, cutting into his flesh with biting stings.

With his head ducked, he tried to find Maddie. In a crouch she moved along the line of bushes near the diving board. She was straight in their line of fire.

But they were aiming at him.

Good. Let them keep coming.

The acrid smell of sulfur filled the air. He listened for screams or sirens but neither came. Grunting and a chorus of moans told him the battle was only starting. So long as the rumbles of pain plagued the other side and not Maddie, he was fine. That meant getting to her and staying mobile enough to reach for safety.

When he looked up, the attacker on the left had changed course. As the other man circled around to the right, this guy headed in a direct line for Maddie. With steady steps and his gun up, the man moved in.

Adam fired off his shots, unloading in the direction of Maddie's biggest threat. The barrage stopped her when she'd sidled only a few feet away. She dropped to the concrete with her hands over her head.

Adam shifted out from his shield and felt a bullet whiz by his head. The heat seared his cheek and he tasted blood on his tongue.

The close call chilled his bones. His hand flew to the shallow scrape near his mouth. It was only a flesh wound. Nothing serious to slow him down.

He grabbed for the second gun near his shoe and immediately reloaded the first. His gunfire kept the attacker to the right pinned against the trees. The one on Adam's left was the problem. He'd dropped to his stomach and followed the path that Maddie had just made. He was within a few feet of grabbing her leg.

Adam spun to the side, diving to the ground and firing a shot. The attacker on the left fell flat to the ground in midlunge.

At the sound, Maddie glanced around, her eyes wide and wild, her hair hanging in her face. She stared at the man who almost had her then scrambled to her feet and started running. She screamed Adam's name as she raced across the patio toward him.

Adam watched her sprint to freedom while he fired at the remaining gunman. Her sneakers smacked against the pavement; her breath whooshed in and out, drowning out the wind.

Adam stepped out to catch her as she hit the patio. The gunman shifted from his hiding place at the same time. With his body in front of hers, Adam shielded her from injury. She screamed as he fired, digging her forehead into his back. Tight together, he shuffled them toward the table as the man pounced.

The only attacker left jumped over a planter filled with dead flowers and edged toward them with his gun aimed at Maddie. Adam landed two shots, hitting what had to be a protective vest. The man did nothing more than flinch. He barely slowed until he was on top of them.

In a face-off, Adam shifted until Maddie was hidden behind him. His size was an advantage. Even if he went down, he could block her as he unloaded his weapons into the man and none of them but Maddie was left standing.

"You can't win this." The temptation to take a shot and aim for the head rushed over Adam.

If it had just been him he would have taken the risk.

But he had Maddie to consider. He had to stay alive long enough to make sure she did.

"I just want the girl," the man said.

Adam tried to place the voice and couldn't. The guy was likely nothing more than a gun for hire. A gun with a fairly accurate shot if the sting on his cheek was any indication.

"That's never going to happen."

"Then we have a problem. You have a gun. I have a gun. But you have a girl to protect and I don't. That gives me the edge."

"I have two guns, so we're even." Adam had more than that, but he let the guy think two.

"So do I."

The laughter in the guy's eyes tipped Adam off. He shot a quick glance in the direction of the attacker he'd downed by the pool. The spot was empty except for an abandoned black glove.

The next thing he felt was a tug at his back and the whip of his weapon being shot out of his right hand.

ONE MINUTE MADDIE was plastered to Adam's back. The next, someone grabbed the back of her shirt and jerked it hard enough to rip the fabric. Blunt fingers jammed into her spine, right in the place once shattered. The shocking pain sent her slamming to her knees.

Her eyes watered and her breath rattled around in her chest. She kneeled in front of her captor as he twisted a thick chunk of her hair in his fist.

She tried to look up at Adam, but the man holding her kept her tight on the ground with his foot on one of her hands. Through her hair she could see Adam holding a gun, shifting from one attacker to the other as he tried to hold them off.

The attacker pulled her hair back until she had no choice but to stare up at him. "I think we have a winner."

She couldn't see their faces through the black coverings they wore, but she saw their eyes. Dead and cold. Clearly, these men relished their jobs as murderers.

"Let her go." A rabid mix of heat and energy pounded off Adam. He was big and strong and totally vulnerable to the two men dressed in full battle gear in front of him.

She knew he wouldn't surrender or back off. For her he'd fight to the death.

"Take me," she said, hoping to give Adam a brief window to survive.

Adam sent her a sharp frown. "Maddie, stop."

"I'm the one you want." She gritted her teeth together when the hold on her hair tightened. "Take me and leave him."

"Now, isn't she accommodating?" joked the one who held her.

She tried to find the breath to speak over the pain. "Knevin wants me, not Adam."

"I don't know who Adam is," the other attacker said as he inched his gun closer to Adam's head. "Is that you?"

She struggled to keep up with the conversation as the dizziness filled her head. Her left leg had gone numb and the wrench in her back morphed into a relentless wave of beating pain.

"Your job is to take me out, right?" Adam looked between the two other men. "Do it and let her go."

The grip on her hair vanished and her head fell forward the second before the guy shoved his hand under her arm. He lifted her to her feet, almost dislocating her shoulder a second time.

"Aren't you two sweet? All willing to die for each other."

"And you both will," the other one said. "Just not together."

Unable to balance herself, she almost fell back in a heap on the concrete until her attacker wrapped his arm around her neck and held her tight to his side. She could smell the sweat on his skin.

Vomit rushed up her throat but she swallowed it back. She needed to stay alert and ready.

"We're going to leave now." The man dragged her across the patio and away from Adam.

"Stop." At Adam's command, she could see her captor's finger twitch on the trigger. "She stays."

"You shoot me, and my friend here will shoot her," her attacker threatened Adam. "You can't win this round." He pulled so tightly on her arm, her shirt collar choked her.

When she started hacking and fighting for breath, Adam's gaze flew to her face. The second off his game cost him. The other attacker kicked out at Adam's chest. She screamed his name as he went down, dropping his gun.

The man holding her laughed. "That was easier than I thought."

The other one kicked Adam in the side, made his body bounce against the ground and his glasses fall. "Guess the reports were wrong. He's not so hard to take down after all."

Ignoring the bruises and pain, she struggled against the guy's hold. Kicking out, she tried to land at least one good shot. But her waning strength was no match for him.

"Stop." He shook her hard enough to rattle her teeth before looking at his partner. "You wanna take care of him?"

The guy stepped on Adam's glasses, smashing them under his heel. "It's no fun if they just pass out first."

"Handle it while I get her ready for transport."

The comment penetrated the terror building inside her. Just as the pieces came together in her mind, her attacker started pulling at her. He tried to drag her away from Adam's sprawled body and her heart shuddered to a stop. "No!"

Hot breath rustled her hair, sending a deadly chill down her spine. "You might not want to watch this part," the gunman whispered in her ear.

Somewhere inside she found the strength

to fight back, like an engine whirling to life. She refused to make it easy.

She hit her attacker's arm with her fists, kicked her feet against his calves. None of it stopped his movements. Furious tears fell down her cheeks and her chest ached from yelling.

When the second attacker stood over Adam with a gun aimed at his head, her heart tore apart. She felt it rip, every part of her body going limp with agonizing grief.

The fight streamed out of her. She fell against her attacker, her stomach rolling and her eyes thick with tears.

"Do it." The order rumbled against her back and echoed in her ear.

The gun lowered to just inches from the back of Adam's head. But just when the attacker laughed at the impending murder and splash of blood, Adam moved. He flipped over and grabbed the weapon, slamming it into the other man's gut.

The guy went down and Adam pounced on him. With grunts and thuds against the ground, they wrestled and fought. If Adam had a problem seeing, he sure didn't show it. The gun fell, clinking against the patio before spinning under a chair.

That left one nearby. She hoped Adam got his hands on it.

Using fists and kicks they scrambled, circling each other, bent over and snarling like wild animals. They lunged and punched. Their bodies moved over the patio to the very edge. Then Adam lost his footing where the patio met the grass, and went down.

"End this thing," the guy holding her raged, all amusement gone from his voice.

Adam lay on his back, moving on his elbows and heels as his attacker stalked. Before the guy could land a final blow, Adam kicked out, catching him in the jaw. The man's head snapped back and his head covering slipped.

One second she caught a glimpse of pale skin and blond hair and the next she stared at Adam's back. He reached down and picked up the other man's body, letting his head loll back and the blood drip off his chin. With one last punch, Adam dropped the guy. He hovered over him with his foot on the man's neck and his fist ready for another pounding.

Just as the fight escalated into a second round, one where Adam held all the power, a shot rent the air. She ducked to escape the gunfire, but at Adam's choked yell, she lifted her head.

His arms out and his mouth open, he fell back in free fall, right into the pool. The splash sent water flying in every direction.

"No!" She tried to run to him, but the guy holding her dug in.

Adam's body sank, slipping under the edge of pool cover where it had separated from the side. A second later, a dark red stream bled into the water.

A cry of anguish hiccuped inside her. She would have fallen on the ground but strong arms held her steady.

The second attacker struggled to his feet. He wiped the blood on his face, turning it into a smear, before slipping the face gear back into place.

"That guy was hard to kill," he said.

Her brain blocked his words. Every cell inside her rebelled at the thought of Adam meeting his horrific end in a pool of dirty water. If she still had any air left in her lungs she would have screamed until she lost her voice.

The man holding her put his cheek next to hers with his tongue practically touching her skin. "Your turn."

She prayed for Adam.

Then she prayed for a quick death.

Chapter Thirteen

Adam tried to move his arms to block the steady thumping against his chest. The muscles across his shoulders ached and his body shook. He heard mumbling. Flashes of light seeped in under his eyelids. He pressed them tighter to block it all out.

Words spilled over him, syllables and sounds he could not identify. Cold pressed in on him and his body shook hard enough to tap his head against something hard and unforgiving underneath him.

Another pound against his chest and the sweet relief of air filled his lungs. He jack-knifed to a sitting position as he gagged on the water filling his mouth. He choked and coughed until his insides fought enough to get out. When he started spitting up yellow bile, he fell to his side and closed his eyes.

"Come on, man."

Zach.

Adam forced his eyes open. The figure sitting next to him blurred. He reached for his glasses but they were gone. A quick rub of his eyes and some of the fog cleared, but the headache didn't.

"About time," Zach said.

Adam noticed his usually unruffled friend gasped as he rubbed a shaky hand down his white face. He was also soaking wet. They both were.

The memories rushed in on Adam, bombarding him until his brain screamed in surrender. The gunmen, the pool. Maddie. He could hear her terrified screams and see her arms reaching for him as he went down.

Where the hell was she?

"Maddie?" He sat up, ignoring every creak and ache. He looked around, his gaze locking on a still man lying in the grass and the blood puddling around him.

He saw a glove, a gun. Broken patio furniture and smashed bushes.

No Maddie.

Zach shifted to his knees with his hands resting on his thighs. "We have to get up."

"I want to see her."

"I know, but I need to make sure you're

okay. There's blood in that pool and I need to know where it's coming from."

The moments underwater came back to Adam slowly. Calling on all his training and keeping his focus on saving Maddie, he'd grabbed a last breath before the water slapped against his skin and closed over his head. He'd hit the surface and kept plunging toward the bottom. No matter how hard he kicked, he couldn't find the surface through the pool cover.

Wrestling a knife from his front pocket, he'd sliced a long cut along his forearm and held his arm up, letting his blood stain the top of the water. If he had any chance of saving Maddie, he needed the attackers to think he was dead. The blood from the gunshot wound he didn't bargain for did the rest.

Less than a minute later his air had run out, taking his endurance with it. His next memory was of Zach's fist banging on his chest.

Adam lifted his arm and investigated his handiwork. The plan had been to flood the water with enough blood to hide the fact that his heart and brain worked just fine. That part worked.

"Come on." Zach stood and reached down

to pull Adam up with him. "We need to get you back to the warehouse and regroup."

It was everything Zach didn't say that had Adam's pulse throbbing in his neck. He stood up and shoved a hand against his friend's shoulder.

"What the—"

Adam willed Zach to understand. "I'm not going anywhere without Maddie."

"There's a hole in your shirt and a cut on your cheek. I see a fresh run of blood dripping down your hand, but I don't know where it's coming from. Could be a cut or a bullet." Those were more words than Zach had spoken all week.

"Tell me she's not dead." Adam searched his mind for a gunshot. Tried to remember if those shocking screams signaled her end.

For every minute during the past few days when he'd tried to push her away or hold her off, he begged now for forgiveness. He wanted her here. He'd apologize about not believing her. He didn't even care about who she was before. He needed the woman she was now.

Zach inhaled, taking his breathing to a normal level as he rested his palms on Adam's shoulders. "She's not here."

"What?"

"Luke is crazed and checking security footage. The cameras picked something up."

"Cameras?"

"We'll follow the car. Right now I'm more concerned with you being shot. The vest did most of the work, but you got more than a nick here."

Adam had bigger issues on his mind. The worry about her being dead was replaced with an equally disturbing realization. Someone had her.

"Zach?"

"We'll trace her. Your system will save her."

All those words and none of them were the ones Adam wanted to hear. "Just tell me."

"They took her."

Maddie felt every bump. When the car turned, she slid across the trunk, banging against the nearest wall and burning her arms against the carpet. With her hands and feet bound, she fought back the urge to scream.

The memory of Adam's face kept playing in her mind. She saw the shock and pain. Watched him slip away forever. That Knevin or whoever had her now thought killing her would cause the most damage was a joke.

They'd destroyed her back on that patio, but not by touching her.

The reserves of strength she'd built up while living alone and learning to rely only on herself had been expelled. She was a woman without a past and now her only shot at a future lay on the bottom of a pool. She didn't even know she wanted the chance until two gunmen stole Adam from her.

She wasn't one to throw around emotions. She didn't believe in love at first sight. But this week taught her about the slow burn. The desire she'd nurtured every day he'd walked into her diner had exploded into a yearning that took over her insular world.

And now he was gone.

The hollow sensation in her chest had swelled to take over her body. She wanted to curl in a ball and refuse to move until Adam magically showed up at her side. To see his face, run her fingers along the hard planes of his shoulders… She'd give anything for those quiet moments she once took for granted.

Tears burned her eyes at the thought of never having that again. It felt as if she had a foot inside her stomach and it kept kicking until she couldn't unclench.

Wallowing in her grief, she hadn't noticed

the car stopped. The trunk flew open before she could ready a plan. The dark night rose above her. She saw stars and a clear sky. The next minute, she saw the masked gunman who had ripped the hair out of her head.

"Get up."

She ignored the order as her brain scrambled to figure out how to use the situation to her benefit. Too late with the answer, she saw him reach in and lift her out of the trunk as if she weighed less than his gun.

"Let me go."

"You know the answer to that."

Her feet hit soft ground. In a rush, she glanced around, trying to memorize her surroundings and find a landmark. The area looked familiar and unfamiliar at the same time. The road cut into the mountain and the steep slope to the ravine below.

She dug in her heels and tried to shift her weight back. "No."

She would not beg. This man would never have the satisfaction of seeing her cry.

"You're switching cars."

Her body went slack. "What?"

"It's not important that you know the details."

Her gaze hit on the headlights behind him.

There were two cars, one on each side of her. Two sets of men, neither of which welcomed her as anything other than an unwanted prisoner. She could make out the shadow of a man standing behind her attacker. The harsh glow of the lights plunged his identity deeper into the darkness beyond.

"What's happening?" she asked.

"We're making the exchange."

The one holding her talked about her as if she were a slab of meat, something to be bartered for and sold. Not a human. The job had Knevin's evil fingerprints all over it. Adam had assured her law enforcement was sitting on Knevin and trying to tie him to new attempts on her life, but even from prison he was making her life impossible in the process.

Shoes crunched against the road. This guy came from the new car. He had stepped out from behind the wheel and walked toward her.

She strained to see her new enemy. A facial expression, hair color—something. Concentrating on the details kept her from obsessing about Adam's fate. Made her forget her probable one.

She waited for the negotiation and switch. They had to say something.

"Here." Her attacker slipped his hand under

her elbow and pushed her toward the darkened figure. "She's your problem now."

The new player didn't say a word. Didn't take another step. His hands remained at his sides and his face stayed hidden.

Her attacker finally let go of her. "Sometime today would be good. My partner needs stitches."

A thrill shot through her. Adam had inflicted damage that she could only hope would be…fatal.

But the quiet now disarmed her. She had trained her mind to shut down and listen. She called on those skills now. Let the men fight and battle. All that mattered to her was getting back to that pool and finding Adam sitting by its side, breathing and alive.

The quiet one handed a thick envelope to her attacker. The move placed the new player in a bath of light for the shortest of seconds. The features weren't familiar.

She'd half expected to see Trevor before she remembered he had men for jobs like this. He wouldn't waste his time on someone he found as unimportant as her.

At least with Trevor she knew her enemy. This new one held out his hand. She tried to stutter her steps and keep from being passed off, but she landed in the new guy's arms.

The old attacker tucked an envelope of cash into his chest pocket. The new one held her tight enough to break her. Neither walked away from their standoff between the car lights. Both remained rooted to the spot on the pavement.

Now that her eyes adjusted, she saw the bigger problem. They both held a gun. Whoever these two were to each other, she didn't sense trust.

Her original attacker nodded toward the car twenty feet away. "Take her and leave."

"Soon."

"What's stopping you?"

The stillness evaporated. The quiet one kept his body flush against her, not moving. Then his arm flew up and a shuddering boom sounded next to her head that rocked through her and made her knees buckle. A second shot shattered the back window of the car that had just held her prisoner.

When the quiet returned she saw a man slumped over her feet and blood sprinkled across her shirt. Looking up, she could see an arm sticking out of the now-open back of the car. Blood assaulted her wherever she turned.

The killings pushed her closer to the edge of sanity. She'd seen so much senseless killing. And all the deaths could be traced back to her.

She looked around, searching the killer's face for an explanation or even a flicker of emotion. If he felt regret he hid it. He was all business. He kicked the gun away from the man on the ground and brought her with him while he checked the pulse on the second slumped body in the car.

By the time they finished and took the envelope back and rounded the hood of the man's car, her survival instinct had rebooted. She separated the aspects of her life. In one compartment she placed her vision of Adam, with him alive and fine. In another she plotted a way out.

She would not die.

"Why kill them?" she asked as her new guard opened the back door and shoved her down on the seat.

He tied together the ropes of her bound hands and feet. The shackles nearly bent her double. It only took seconds for her back to cry out in a new flash of pain.

She couldn't sit up or separate her hands from her feet. She was bound and controlled and neutralized.

Just when she switched from trying to engage the man to controlling the pain, he finally spoke. "It's simple."

"What is?"

"No witnesses."

She knew that included her.

Chapter Fourteen

"We'll get her back, man." Caleb made the comment as he finished the last stitch on Adam's arm.

Bloody gauze and an open medical kit, its contents spilling out, sat next to Adam. He wanted to lash out and knock it all to the floor.

He didn't need anesthesia because he couldn't feel anything anyway. His body, his heart, it was all numb. A minor wound on his face and an insignificant shot through the fleshy part of his upper arm didn't warrant this level of concern. The arm pounded as it swelled, but it was a nuisance only.

He glanced at the faces lined up around the conference room table. Clearly Caleb had sounded the alarm and they all came running. Even the women showed up for this one. Luke had eased their lockdown back at his house and brought them along.

Adam appreciated the show of support, but their energy was misplaced. They should be running scenarios and looking at tape. Time was running out for Maddie…if it hadn't expired already.

Claire rubbed her growing belly with a look of dark menace in her eyes. "It will all be okay. Don't worry."

Adam wasn't in the mood for any of this. They were wasting time and sitting in the wrong state. That Caleb had brought him back to D.C., actually knocked him out with a shot despite his promise of retaliation, ticked Adam off.

If Avery were the one missing, Caleb would be racing through the woods to find her. They all would. In the past, they did. Adam wanted the same red-alert scramble for Maddie.

He was done with the nursing and babying. "Let me up."

Luke pressed a hand against Adam's chest, holding him down. "Not an option."

Adam shoved the arm away and threw his legs over the side of the table. His brain followed a step behind. When a wave of nausea rolled over him, he closed his eyes to keep from falling down. One show of weakness and he'd never get out of there and back to Rod's house to search for clues.

"The people looking for Maddie need her dead." The word hung there. He couldn't say more until he wrestled his emotions back under control. "That means she has an expiration date and it could be now."

"I understand."

"Do you?

"Yes." Luke pointed at Claire.

He didn't say the words, but the reference to Claire's previous near-death experience came through. She'd outrun the police and a crazed ex-husband. She'd survived with Luke's help, and Luke had the limited use of one arm to prove it.

The memory took the edge off Adam's anger, but the welling anxiety remained. "Look, I know—"

Luke cut him off. "They took her. I get that, but they didn't kill her."

"Am I supposed to be grateful?"

"You should realize that them waiting means something and buys us time to figure out what."

Holden stepped up to the table. His usual joking demeanor had been replaced with an intensity that pulsed like a living creature. "We tracked the car via satellite and surveillance cameras. Zach is at the spot now. The guys who attacked you are dead and there are signs of a scuffle."

Adam felt a flash of unrealistic hope. "Maddie?"

"She's not there. There are tracks for another car, so it looks like a shoot-and-grab."

As the information dipped back into horror, Adam's belief in bringing her out alive waned. He'd already forced out of his mind the horrible images of Maddie being hurt or worse. He held on to a thin sliver of hope but he was losing the grip.

He didn't know how to fight an enemy he couldn't name. This thing ran so deep, was so entrenched and dangerous. It was as if they'd gotten caught between warring groups of corruption. But he had no idea who led the armies.

Caleb repacked the medical kit. "This can't all be Trevor."

"I'm not sure any of it is."

Luke was wrong on that. Adam knew. He could feel the twist in his gut every time Trevor's name was mentioned. The fact that the man lived and thrived while Maddie faced danger was a constant reminder to Adam of

Recovery's failure. With each second he lost faith in Rod and their ability to end this nightmare with Maddie beside them.

As far as Adam could tell, bargaining with the devil wasn't working. Trevor needed to feel the slice and sting, to know his life could be snatched away, before he'd help.

Holden held up a contacts case. "You might need these."

"Only to see." Adam folded it in his palm. "What now?"

"Zach is trying to track the second car," Luke explained.

Adam caught the note of doubt in Luke's voice. "You don't think it will work."

"The area was pretty rural and not a location we can depend on for a lot of feeds."

Adam appreciated the truth, but he wasn't sure where that left them. If anywhere.

When no one interrupted or asked a question, Luke continued. "We run a search on the dead men and see if we can trace them back to someone. Caleb and Avery will check any forensics."

It was a solid playbook and if they had more time and a few more leads, maybe it would pan out. But as Luke described it, the plan would never work.

Adam said the words that wouldn't leave his head. "They are going to kill her."

Mia patted his good arm. "You don't know that."

They didn't know. They didn't see Maddie flinch or feel the hard knots under her skin. He had. "She's already injured and vulnerable."

"Adam Wright, stop it." Claire's hands moved to her hips. "Maddie is one of the most self-sufficient women I've ever met. She fought you off. She escaped that Knevin person. She didn't melt into a puddle when gunmen arrived. She gave up everything to live. And all of that shows she's a fighter."

But Adam knew the one thing the men standing with him understood and the women wanted to forget. "Maddie can't outrun a bullet."

"Okay." Luke clapped his hands. "This isn't helping. We're going to check in with Zach and get started."

Adam had another plan. Not one he could share or depend on Luke to support. He didn't blame Luke for that. He was the leader and had to think of the safety of the team and preserve some amount of cover for them. He was responsible.

Adam's plan wasn't. It was reckless and bordered on irrational. But it was Maddie's only hope.

He held up the contacts case and went into the bathroom. After he put them in, he started the countdown. Armed only with his watch and his administrator capabilities, he disabled the building's alarm system.

The cloak of security would be down long enough for him to slip out. He'd have only minutes to get to his car and out of the lot. He didn't want their headquarters vulnerable for any longer than necessary.

If any of them concentrated on the security cameras instead of their assigned tasks, they'd see his trick. If not, the infinite loop would give him a short period of cover.

There were exactly two ways out of the building. The obvious one was the door and Luke guarded it as if he knew Adam planned to make a break. The other was the escape hatch in the back corner under the stairs. Always have two ways in and out was Luke's rule.

The space was tight and uncomfortable, and in his current banged-up condition he doubted he could fold his body small enough to get in there. But he would do it somehow.

He stepped out of the bathroom and all eyes went to him. Just as he expected. His team was smart enough to know he wouldn't accept this plan without a fight.

Holden broke the silence. "I could use your help tracking the car."

Adam glanced down at the mix of blood and mud caked on his shirt. "Let me change first."

A stare burned into the back of his shirt as he walked, probably from Luke, but no one tried to stop him. When Adam made a show of digging through the stack of clothes he kept here, the buzz of conversation returned.

A quick look through the slats of the stairs and he saw his moment. His team shuffled around, looking at documents and videos. Caleb and Avery huddled over a feed coming in from Zach.

It was ten minutes before Luke noticed Adam was gone.

MADDIE CAME AWAKE with a sharp intake of breath. Her head popped up through the black void in which she'd been swimming, and she gasped. Afraid to move, she looked around. She didn't have to guess her location. Everything was familiar because she sat in the middle of the living room in her West Virginia cabin.

She tried to move her arm, but cables tied her to a chair and some sort of band forced her wrists together behind her back. She couldn't kick or get the leverage to slide. They—and she had no idea who "they" even were—had locked her ankles to the thin wooden spindles of her dining room chair.

Gray clouds blocked the world outside her window. The overcast weather fit the mood and desperation of the situation. Inside the cabin wasn't any brighter. The lights were off, making the room cool and dark. She didn't know what time it was or how long she'd been out, but she guessed it was early morning.

She could smell the rain in the mountains, feel the incoming storm at the base of her sore back as she always did. There was no sign of the men from the cars or of Trevor or of any of the people she remembered from Knevin's circle.

The one person she wanted to see was the one face she blocked. If she let her mind wander to what could have happened to Adam and where he was now, she'd lose it. Right now she needed all her strength and determination.

Bringing her here was their one mistake.

She knew this house. She'd practiced drills and worked on endless escape scenarios. If her back held out, she could get to the roof or crawl through the tunnel to the shed. She'd still be miles from safety, but she'd have a chance. From there she could fight.

But she had to get loose first.

She twisted her hands, trying to wrench free. The bindings rubbed a heated burn across her skin but didn't break. They were too tight. Her shoulders were strapped down and her fingers useless. They grew numb from lack of circulation.

She glanced around for anything that could help. Whoever held her had moved all the furniture to the sides of the room. Nothing was close. All the sharp objects and glasses were missing. She couldn't saw through the cables with a pillow or gnaw through them with her teeth, so she had to come up with something.

She looked around the room. On the opposite wall was a small clock. She'd gotten it free when she'd taken her car into the garage for a brake job. It was ugly, with a logo of a cartoon car. Right now it was her favorite possession.

She needed to smash the glass. If she was able to knock life into her fingers, she could try to cut through whatever held her hands together.

After listening for movement or voices and hearing only the usual life in the woods, she got started. She rocked her body back and forth. On the third tip forward, the chair crashed to the hardwood. Unable to brace for the landing, she fell with a hard smack against her previously injured shoulder.

The impact knocked the breath from her body and vibrated through her. She didn't feel any pain. She was past the point of bruises. The muscles in her legs jumped involuntarily and her skin prickled.

She shook her head and inhaled several times to jump-start herself after the spill. On her side, she shimmied her way across the floor.

The task took what felt like hours.

Spanning the ten feet exhausted her, robbed her of every last ounce of strength. But giving up was not an option. She thought about Adam and never having the chance to tell him how much she cared for him, and she felt a flare of energy that keep her arms and legs moving. She bent at the waist, ignoring the new shock of squealing pain radiating down her legs. With her feet as close to her chest as the cables would allow, she tucked and then pushed her legs out. Her ankles slammed into the wall. She repeated the move over and over until her muscles shook and her legs went numb.

The clock bobbled. The sides rattled against the soft green walls. The noise cracked like fireworks in the small space.

She hesitated, waiting for her attackers to come running, but nothing happened. The only sound she heard was the swift winds swaying the branches outside.

After one last countdown, she wound up and shot her feet out again. The smack jarred her bones, but it worked. The clock bounced against the wall and fell. It clanked as it rolled to a stop. The glass splintered but didn't break.

"Yes!" She didn't realize she'd been grinding her teeth together until she relaxed her jaw and the soreness in her gums eased.

Now she had to break it.

She balanced most of her weight against the back of the chair. When she rocked forward, the leg hammered into the cracked glass. The clock skidded across the room as pieces of the shattered glass went flying.

She flipped to her stomach to shift the chair closer to the shards. The bits crunched under her. The sharp edges cut into her chest through her shirt.

Swinging the bottom of the chair around, her fingers lined up with the glass pieces. She reached out for one, when she heard a thud near her head.

She froze.

Glancing over, she saw black shoes and dark pants. Her gaze moved higher, but she couldn't see anything from this position. She didn't have to. Terror ripped through her when she realized she wasn't alone in the room.

A deep chuckle filled the silence. "If you wanted me to cut you, you only had to ask."

Chapter Fifteen

Sela ran after Adam as he stalked through the quiet private hallway of Trevor's company, Orion, two hours before the building opened to the public. He'd come in before six thinking the hallways would be abandoned. Turned out Trevor had full staff on at all times.

Adam had used his fallback plan. He'd shut down the internal security cameras a few minutes before. Knocking out the guys manning the monitors and typing right on the keyboard had proven faster and easier than hacking his way in. He hadn't had time for routing and proxy servers. The butt of his gun had worked fine.

Just proved that walking into a building as if you belonged there worked better than any subterfuge. He'd made it the whole way to the basement level before anyone tried to stop him. That guy was curled up in a bathroom stall right now. His headache would last at least a day.

Adam had ripped open the door to the outer office of the suite and spied Sela's desk. Small room, big desk. It was a nice setup for a boss who wanted to enjoy some quiet time with his assistant.

Now Sela slid in front of Adam as he reached for the door to Trevor's inner office. "You can't go in there."

"But I am." He wore a T-shirt and carried a gun. A smart woman would know he wasn't all that concerned with rules and restrictions.

She frowned at him. "You need an appointment."

Adam looked her over. He couldn't figure out if she was brave or stupid. She certainly seemed prepared to sacrifice her life for Trevor. That meant one thing: this was not the usual boss-secretary relationship. Not the kind Human Resources bragged about in sexual-harassment seminars.

Finding a hot blonde in Trevor's outer office wasn't a surprise. Adam assumed pretty women with big breasts went with the wealth-and-power routine. This one looked a bit young, but it wasn't his business.

He put his hand on Sela's arm and pushed

her to the side and away from the doorknob. "You should leave."

"I can't let you—" Her gaze lit on his gun.

Adam knew then she hadn't seen it before. That explained the show of bravado.

"Don't hurt him." She whispered the plea.

"Your boyfriend will be fine."

"He's my boss."

"Call him whatever you want. I'm going in."

Fear played on every part of her from her trembling lips to her nervous hands. "I called security."

He knew that was a lie. He'd been right next to her since he hit the floor. They'd ridden up on the elevator together, her balking when he got off on the security-restricted floor. "Congratulations on following office procedure."

"You should leave while you can."

"You either need to move or shoot me. But either way, I'm going in that door." He pointed at Trevor's nameplate.

"I can't."

"Do I look like a man who is playing around here?"

"Please." All the color leeched out of her already pale skin.

Adam almost felt sorry for her. He didn't want to terrorize her. It was not his style. "Do yourself a favor and only sacrifice yourself for someone who's worth it. This guy isn't."

The door opened in front of Adam. Trevor stood there in a black designer suit and bright blue tie. No weapon. No worry on his face. He possessed his usual cool detachment.

Sela snapped out of her stupor. "Mr. Walters, I tried—"

"It is fine, Sela. I have been watching our guest since he walked in the building. He disabled the building's cameras but not my private feed."

"Security is on the way."

Trevor waved her off. "We will not need any help."

Her eyes widened. "Sir, he has a gun."

"Probably more than one, but I am willing to bet Mr. Wright needs something from me. If so, he can ill afford to shoot me."

"Your ego will get you killed one of these days," Adam muttered.

Trevor pushed open his door and drew out a hand, indicating Adam should step inside. "I could say the same thing about you. It takes quite a bit of…shall we say, confidence, to barge in here with a gun strapped to your side."

Adam had no intention of giving Trevor his

back. He used the weapon to wave the other man into the office first then clicked the lock behind them. He knew Sela was even now screaming for security to come running.

"I'm happy to see you understand what's happening here, Trevor."

"I am more concerned with how you got through security and how easily you disposed of my men and video cover." Trevor stood behind his desk, flipping his pen between his fingers. "I see some additional training is in order on my end."

"Shut up."

Trevor smiled. "And here I was being friendly."

"Stop talking."

"Fine. Tell me why you are here, Adam."

"Give Maddie back."

The pen hung loose from his fingers. "Are you saying you lost your woman?"

"If I get her back safe and unhurt, you get to live. Any other condition, you die." Adam didn't move from his spot. He stood, legs apart, right in front of Trevor's desk.

Face-to-face, Adam was able to see every move. If Trevor reached for a gun, Adam was prepared to shoot his arm. He'd keep firing until he got the information he needed.

Trevor hesitated, and the tension in the room increased to suffocating proportions. "You do realize you are in my office."

"Yes."

"That security is right now storming up here and waiting for my order to break in."

"And you are well aware of how good a shot I am and that I'm not afraid of dying." Adam raised the gun, aiming at Trevor's forehead.

"If you do this, you lose everything."

"So do you, starting with your life, and I can live with that."

"I do not have your girlfriend."

Adam didn't bother to deny the relationship. That's exactly what she was, or what she would be once he got her back and explained that her running days were over.

"I am going to start shooting in ten seconds."

"Maybe you should wait for Luke."

"What?"

Trevor held up his hands as if waiting for permission to move again. When Adam nodded, Trevor turned one of the three monitors on his desk to face Adam. "As I said, there's more than one monitoring system in the building. Using mine I believe you can see that is him in the elevator."

Luke and Holden stood there, staring at the floor panel. Adam couldn't see the weapons in the grainy video but knew both were carrying.

"I see the entire Recovery team is suffering from a serious lack of control," Trevor said.

"This isn't about them. This is about you and me. They won't stop me from killing you."

"I believe Luke is smarter than that."

"I'm running this one."

Sela's voice sounded over the intercom. "Sir, you have visitors."

Trevor touched a button on the phone. "Send the Recovery men in. Security should stand down."

"Sir—"

"No one comes in unless I say so. They can wait in the kitchen."

Adam knew a code word when he heard one. "Kitchen?"

"The safety word. The one that guarantees my men don't kill you when that door opens or rappel through the window."

Adam shifted around to Trevor's side of the desk. He pressed the gun against Trevor's temple as he glanced outside. When he was satisfied an attack wasn't imminent, he nodded at Trevor to open the door. With a touch of his keyboard, the door unlocked.

"Nice trick."

Trevor held his body stiff. "You are not the only tech expert in town."

The door opened only wide enough for a body to slide through. Luke came in, gun raised. Holden followed, though he was focused on something behind them in the hall.

"Welcome." Trevor looked sideways in Adam's direction. "You can lower the gun now. This breach is between me and Luke."

Holden remained by the door, but Luke stepped up to take Adam's abandoned position at the desk. "I'm thinking about letting Adam shoot you."

Adam watched his friends. Neither showed any reaction other than unconditional support for the stunt at the warehouse and the bold move of coming there. In private they'd likely blast him, but they were a united front right now.

The frustration inside him broke loose. "I want Maddie."

"I told you, I don't—" Trevor swallowed back his words when Adam shoved the gun hard against his skin. "I see."

"Tell the man what he wants to know," Luke said.

"I did not take her."

Adam refused to ease up. "But you know who did."

Trevor tucked his pen in his inside jacket pocket. "Maybe we can make a new deal."

Adam felt the tension in the room shift. Trevor no longer held on to the fake sense of outrage at being accused. He'd moved into bargaining mode, which was exactly the plan.

"You've already violated the old agreement," Luke said.

"Not true."

"It is by my reading."

Trevor pursed his lips. "There might be details I could assume for you."

Luke rolled his eyes. "That's nice of you."

"My name would have to stay clear. Anything you found that referenced me or my company, or anyone associated with either, would have to remain between us."

"You want us to grant you immunity."

"As I have stated, I have not committed a crime."

Adam was done with the verbal swordplay. "Luke, we're running out of time here."

"You should listen to your computer genius." Trevor gave Adam a dismissive look. "While he appears to be out of control at the moment, he is not wrong about the timeline."

Luke looked at Adam and then Holden. When he turned back to Trevor, Luke wore an expression of grim determination. "Accepted."

Adam blew out the breath he was holding. He hadn't realized how important Luke's answer was until he said it.

"Lower the gun," Trevor ordered in a flat tone.

Adam pulled back but did not take Trevor out of his sights. "Talk."

"If I were in charge of this operation, there is only one place I would take your Ms. Timmons." Trevor paused as if waiting for them to beg for the information. When that didn't happen, he continued. "Back to the last home she had. The house in West Virginia."

"Why?" Luke asked.

"An accident is much easier to stage there. It's consistent with the original plan, which likely had been in preparation for months." Trevor's attention focused on Adam. "And who is going to care about the accidental death of a waitress, sometimes cook, in a dead-end, off-the-grid town?"

Despite the rise of hatred in his blood, Adam didn't take the bait. "So, she's alive?"

"I cannot guarantee that. But I believe, if we were in charge of a money scheme like the one at WitSec, we would want to gather as much information as possible before eliminating all threats. Otherwise a new one could pop up without warning."

It's what Trevor didn't say that made Adam nervous. "Information about what?"

"The final loose end."

Adam toyed with the idea of shooting Trevor just to see him lose some of that unbelievable ego. "What are you talking about?"

"I assume you will follow this case until it ends, no matter where it ends, correct?"

"Except for the deal we made here earlier and the one before that, which let you off the hook." Luke nodded. "Yeah."

"Then that leaves one loose end." Trevor took time staring at all of them. "The Recovery Project."

The sharp silence lasted long enough to get Adam thinking. They'd spent the past year fighting off people who wanted to destroy them. That might be the only life he had from now on.

"Okay." Luke tucked his gun in his belt. "We'll see if you're correct."

Trevor's eyebrow lifted. "Excuse me?"

"Holden is going to stay here with you for a few hours."

Trevor sat down at his desk. "Absolutely not."

Adam still didn't trust the man not to hit a button that brought the ceiling down on them. He focused his aim as he issued his order. "Hands."

Luke waited for Trevor to comply before talking. "The last time I thought we had a deal and you sent in men to help me, Caleb and Avery nearly got killed."

"Not by me."

"No, your men were too busy killing Russell, the one witness who could have given us the WitSec information we needed and kept Maddie safe months ago. You protected your reputation and incidentally kept the corruption going when you took Russell out."

"He was a dangerous man," Trevor said.

"So are you," Adam retorted.

Luke talked over both of them. "Holden will make sure you don't make any calls to partners or anyone else related to what's happening in West Virginia."

Trevor slowly lowered his elbows to his desk. "You have a trust issue."

"I wonder why." Luke looked at Adam and nodded in the direction of the door. "Trevor, we walk out of here and no one touches us, right?"

"Yes."

"Because if that doesn't happen, I'm going to kill you," Adam said.

Holden stepped forward, his attention focused on Trevor. "And while they're driving we can talk."

Trevor opened a folder and stared at it. "I do not think so."

Holden balanced his hip against the corner of Trevor's desk and ignored the furious glare he got in response. "Okay. I'll talk and you can listen."

Adam waited at the door for Luke to join him. Adam wasn't the type to drop a lot of apologies. He operated straight and focused on work. That left little room for trouble.

"Look, I—"

Luke held up his hand. "No need to explain." Adam searched his friend's face for anger and didn't find it. "You realize because of me and what I just did we can't touch Trevor."

He glanced at the man in question then turned back. "You have to pick your fights, Luke. I pick Maddie over Trevor."

Adam had always had priorities. For a long time, only the Recovery team, along with

Claire, Mia and Avery, held those spots. Now Maddie had moved onto the list. To the top of it.

"Why aren't you furious?" he asked Luke.

Luke took out his gun and signaled to Holden to provide cover in case Trevor was working another con. "Because I know what I'd do if someone had Claire."

"I appreciate that."

For the first time all day, Luke smiled. "What, you're not going to tell me how this is different because I love Claire and married her, and you're just watching over Maddie?"

Adam didn't hesitate. "No."

Chapter Sixteen

The man circled her. Every inch of Maddie's skin crawled at his presence, but she tried not to move. She didn't know who he was, but she despised him.

Lying there, still tied to a chair, she was completely vulnerable to him. And she couldn't even see his face.

Black unscuffed shoes thumped against the floor, stopping behind her. She felt her last chance at freedom slip away when glass crunched beneath his feet.

"You could have hurt yourself," he said.

She didn't recognize the deep voice and didn't bother responding. She needed him to talk. The more time he wasted, the better chance for her to come up with a way out.

He grabbed the chair and with a grunt lifted her to a sitting position. The inside of her head continued to rock even after the chair stilled.

She'd kept her body toned and in shape with long runs. The goal was to stay in good condition to handle stress and increase her chances of getting away if needed. But all the injuries over the past few days were adding up. Her shoulder ached and her muscles functioned now only thanks to a rush of adrenaline and the fuel of fear.

When her head stopped rattling, she looked up at her captor. She expected some recognition but had none. His dark, short hair was nothing unusual. In his black suit he looked like every businessman in D.C. This guy could fit in any upper-middle-class neighborhood and no one would know about his killing instincts.

If life were fair, the evil ones would give off a vibe to warn women to run. "Who are you?" she asked him.

"That's not important."

"Since you want me dead it's a big deal to me."

There was no way Knevin hired this guy. Knevin wasn't the type to hang out with guys who cared about retirement accounts and stock portfolios.

"You've caused me a great deal of trouble."

The man paced back and forth in front of her as he talked.

"You'll have to narrow it down a little."

"You're supposed to be dead."

"Several people have tried to make that happen. No one has been successful."

"Yet."

She twisted her hands. The bindings gave a little more than before, though she couldn't shift her shoulders or break free. She had to figure out a way to convince this guy to loosen the restraints.

He took a few more steps. "And you violated the rules."

She stopped fidgeting. "What rules?"

"Witness protocol is very clear. When you ran to the Recovery Project, you became another sad statistic."

He was with WitSec. The fact hit her like a blow to the head. It all made sense. He was high up somewhere, likely above Russell, and knew all about her.

"You'd think a woman with your past would appreciate the opportunity you were given to start over." He stopped in front of her, so close she had to wrench her neck to see his face. "Instead, like so many before you and countless others who will follow, you broke with the plan."

The guy didn't even know her and he hated her. His disgust wrapped around every word. The snarl and angry tone just highlighted how insignificant and unworthy he found her to be.

She'd gotten that from men her entire life. As if being poor made a person unlovable. That need for male acceptance drove her right to Knevin, a man who claimed to love her and only gave her pain.

Well, no more. She deserved better and was not about to let some piece of garbage in a suit talk down to her. If she was going to die, she'd go out on her terms.

"Your men were trying to kill me. I did what I had to do to survive."

"The statistics are clear. Participants stay safe unless they break with protocol." He droned on as if giving a speech.

"What are you talking about?"

He crossed his arms over his chest. "That's what I'll explain when I testify behind the closed doors of the congressional committee concerning the spate of recent deaths in WitSec. The program has a perfect record so long as the participants follow the rules. When they contact their old criminal friends or do one of the many things they're told not to do, they risk the lives of the U.S. Marshals who are trying so hard to protect them."

"I didn't do any of that."

"But why is anyone surprised? You know what they say, once a criminal..."

"Who are you?" This time there was anger in her voice.

"The man who makes the decisions."

"I don't—" She saw movement through the window next to the front door. She tried not to focus on it, to just glance in case the light and shadow belonged to help.

The man laughed. "Don't get excited. He's one of mine."

Her lungs deflated. "Good for you."

"Before you become a statistic, I need you to answer some questions."

"No."

"While I might not believe in hurting women, my men will not hesitate. You might want to keep that in mind before being flip."

Her stomach tumbled at the threat, but she held her expression still. "I assume you think you're above it? Well, let me tell you something. You're worse than them because you don't even have the guts to roll up those sleeves and do the job yourself."

His teeth slammed together right before he backhanded her. Her neck snapped as her head fell to the side and her hair fell across her face. She was about to sit up and face him down again when she saw it. The small door in the hallway moved. It opened a few inches then closed again.

Adam.

It was impossible and unlikely, but she felt the truth through every cell. He'd lived and figured out where she was and how to get to her. He knew about the makeshift escape route.

He needed cover to get in without being detected. And she'd provide it.

She sat back up and screwed her lips in a look filled with her revulsion for the guy in front of her. "Did that make you feel like a man?"

"Do not test me."

"Maybe that's what you need to feel good. Is that right?"

"You would be wise to keep your mouth shut."

"You want a woman to smack around so you can hide how incompetent…or should I say, impotent, you are."

He grabbed her shoulders and shook her.

Hate spewed out of him. He called her names and promised her a slow death.

She took it all. Seeing Adam's shoulders peek out of the closet gave her the strength to take anything. On his hands and knees now, he moved with the grace of a panther and as quiet as smoke.

He was halfway out when a figure appeared in the opening to the bedroom behind him. Adam stopped midcrawl.

"Looks like we have company," the figure said.

At the sound of the voice, the guy in the suit spun around. All attention went to the small hallway.

The figure kicked out, taking advantage of Adam's position on his knees and hands. When the swift kick to the stomach knocked Adam to the floor, a scream died in her throat. Seeing Adam down, his face turned toward her and his eyes closed, sapped the rest of her strength. She felt the hit against her ribs as if she'd been the victim.

"Search him for weapons," the man in the suit said. He leaned down until his face floated right in front of her. "Do you still think I'm weak?"

TREVOR LOOKED OVER THE TOP of his folder and eyed Holden. "I would assume your assistance is needed in West Virginia."

Holden sat with his feet propped up on the corner of the desk. He held his gun and never looked away from Trevor. "I'm fine here, but thanks for your fake concern."

"If you came on with me at Orion you could take on more of a leadership role."

"Really?"

In Trevor's experience, all men had a price. It was a matter of finding it and making the offer. "A man with your skills and background would thrive in my company. I could limit your travel and risks. You are a strategy man and that is always in demand."

Holden blinked. "I meant, are you really trying to sell that garbage to me?"

"You have a purpose now. Responsibilities and a future." Trevor tapped his pen against his open palm. The answer was to go straight to Holden's weakness. "I know Mia has refused to set a date for the marriage, but having a stable income could help push her in the right direction. Women need stability."

A muscle in Holden's jaw twitched, but his voice stayed even. "And you know that from your divorce counseling?"

It looked as if Holden's tipping point would be harder to find. "It is a matter of vision. Looking into the future and setting your course toward a goal."

"You know what I can't figure out?"

Trevor was not naive enough to believe he had changed Holden's mind. The man was playing, searching for information. Trevor really could not blame Holden for doing what came naturally.

"Have we finished talking about future prospects?" Trevor asked.

"You have everything—the power, the solid reputation, the son, the million-dollar company." Holden's gaze traveled around the room, landing on photographs and objects as he talked.

"Your point?"

"How does a guy who built all that get wrapped up in a scheme to earn quick cash by knocking off WitSec participants?"

"I had nothing to do with the deaths of those women in the WitSec program. I didn't sell the information about their location or pull the trigger."

"You say that like you believe it."

In Trevor's mind it was true. He had been dragged in by Russell and Bram. That the operation went deeper and higher, that John decided to engage in blackmail, could not be seen as Trevor's responsibility. He refused to take that on.

Trevor decided it was time to plant the seed. He had not been lying when he talked about loose ends. John Tate was one. Tate's unknown partner was another. If Trevor could arrange for the Recovery team to trim away those dangerous pieces he'd view his plan as a success.

He just had to get them running in that direction first. Sending them to grab John under the guise of rescuing Maddie Timmons was the first piece. When the partner rose up, Trevor would send Recovery after that person, too, even if it was one of their own.

The blackmail tape would become another part of the deal with Recovery. They were really helping cover up two problems, not one.

"Have you ever made a mistake, Holden?"

Holden sighed. "Look, if you're asking for forgiveness it's not going to happen."

"This is not my battle."

"You're involved."

"Not by choice."

Holden sat up straighter. "What does that mean?"

Trevor almost smiled when Holden took

the bait. "It is really a matter of finding an end. John Tate is not the top of this. He was career civil service but under too close a level of scrutiny to pull this off alone. And Russell was an idiot. A follower only."

"Who is the leader?"

"I honestly do not know."

"Did you really just use the word *honestly?*"

Trevor leaned forward on his elbows. "Do you think I would continue on this road if I did not have to?"

A smile crossed Holden's lips. "What do they have on you?"

"It will not be that easy."

"So, there is something." Holden glanced at his watch. Whatever he saw there made him frown. "You have to know where else we should look."

"Think in terms of who else has access. I did not kidnap Ms. Timmons, but someone with connections and financing did." Trevor tapped his fingertip against the desk. "You should ask yourself who is in a position to have information on the WitSec participants and the funding necessary to make the plan work."

"That's a lean list."

"Look at the details no one should have

known and then figure out who other than the Recovery agents did."

"You mean Vince."

Trevor was impressed once again. Looked as if the Recovery members had started questioning their own. It was smart to be cautious. "Or Rod."

Holden's mouth flatlined. "He's missing."

"Are you sure?"

Chapter Seventeen

"Banner, pull him in here. I'm sure Maddie would like to say goodbye to her boyfriend."

Adam kept his eyes closed and his body loose as the goon named Banner pulled him across the floor. Banner yanked hard enough to pull his shoulders out of their sockets, but Adam didn't make a noise. He spent the time inventorying his remaining weapons.

Banner got both guns and a knife. That left one knife and his secret weapons: Zach and Luke.

When Adam's head smacked against the floor, he hid a wince. Not exactly the heroic way he wanted to get to Maddie, but he was inside. And she was alive. Bruised and fighting hard enough to get herself killed, but alive.

When he'd sat cramped in that metal tube, he'd worked the fake panel loose without letting it crash onto the floor and give him away.

Hearing Maddie's voice made him work faster and more efficiently.

He had so much to say to her, so much he wanted to do with her. That all depended on getting out of the tiny space.

Listening to John Tate talk about Recovery almost ruined the game. Adam had wanted to race through the tedious work and come out firing. But Maddie's safety mattered more than speed. More than taking revenge on Tate. More than uncovering the final pieces of the WitSec scheme.

Adam would have blown it all if he thought he could get through the door without running into one of John's goons. They were all over the property. Zach had been tracking them and decided these weren't Trevor's men. These guys were trained but didn't work together. They were individual mercenaries and in this business that made all the difference. A team had to be in sync and this one wasn't.

Adam was willing to bet one of them was being paid to kill all the others when this operation was done. No way was John leaving a loose end who could identify him. He probably planned to be the only one standing by the time the night was done.

Adam had another scenario in mind. When

Banner dumped him, faceup in front of Maddie's chair, he went to work. His head was half under her and both arms were tucked out of sight. One hand landed by her foot, close enough to work on the binding around her ankle.

His fingers brushed against her. A finger slipped up her pant leg to brush against her skin. When she stiffened then relaxed, he knew she got the message. He wasn't dead or even unconscious. He was there for her.

With small movements, he tugged at the cable. To get her out of there, he first had to get her out of the chair. He could pass her to Luke, who would drive her to safety no matter how much she protested. She could beg and Luke would stay focused.

That was the promise Adam had insisted on when they stopped the car a half mile up the road. If he went down, they would leave him to save her. Luke had only agreed when Adam mentioned Claire's name. Zach never said the words.

Still, every scenario they talked through depended on getting her outside.

"You failed." Adam could hear the smile in Maddie's voice as she said the words.

John shifted until he stood right over

Adam's sprawled body. "You are tied up and your boyfriend is out cold. I am ten minutes away from having this entire mess wrapped up. So, Maddie, tell me how I lost."

"It's easy and obvious."

"Yes?"

"Your men didn't kill Adam at Rod's house as you thought. He's been alive all this time. He knew to come here to find me. Don't you wonder about that?"

"No."

"You don't even care that you may have been followed?"

"I wasn't." John's sure words didn't match the shakiness of his tone.

"Someone tipped Adam off to your intentions. He got through whatever command post you have set up outside and walked right into this house."

"He crawled."

"Doesn't matter since it happened right around you and your men and you didn't even notice. Whatever security you have out there isn't working."

Keep talking. Adam mentally sent that message to her.

She made him proud. She got John keyed up and kept the focus on her while Adam worked.

She was the perfect partner. Smart and capable.

"A small setback only, but we're back on track," John said.

Adam freed her first ankle. She could kick, which gave them one more weapon. He slid his hand by fractions of an inch until it rested next to her other foot.

His fingers were damp from what he guessed was a mix of sweat and blood. Each time the cable bit into his skin, he fought off a flinch and remembered Maddie's face. He owed her whatever injuries he sustained. He'd failed to keep her safe.

"You still don't get it." Maddie laughed as she talked.

"You seem determined to tell me." John shifted his weight until his foot pressed against Adam's side. "Go ahead."

"Do you honestly think Adam kept his mouth shut during the time between then and now? That he hasn't told everyone that you are behind this?" Maddie's voice grew stronger with every word.

Adam could feel the mood of the room shift from tension to confidence. But not for everyone. John continued to argue, but his stance changed. He moved around, growing more agitated as she talked.

Damn, he loved her.

It didn't make sense and the timing was all wrong, but Adam felt it. He just hoped he lived long enough to tell her.

John's hands fisted at his sides. "Adam couldn't have known that until right now."

"You can't be that clueless." Maddie snorted. "Adam has connections in government, with the police. He has an entire team at his disposal. He is a computer genius and can get access to private information in a second."

Adam freed Maddie's second foot and none too soon. Much more of this prodding and she would get herself shot. He glanced up through half-closed eyes to figure out how much room he had to move.

He called up his mental blueprint of the room and placed the players in it. John was right on top of him and Banner stood ten feet away.

There were others outside, roaming the grounds and guarding the door, but Zach was handling them. With his injury, Luke took the communications job and relayed positions to Zach.

Banner was the problem. He stood just far

enough away to make a running lunge at him impossible. He also held all the guns, and if that kick was any indication, the guy had a serious anger problem. Adam's kidneys had shriveled at the contact. He knew he'd see blood in his urine for weeks.

"You still don't know who I am," John said.

"I really don't care."

John closed in on her. He rested his hands on the chair, trapping her in the seat. "I'm John Tate."

"And?"

"You talk about the government, well, I am one of Adam's government contacts. I am the one with power and access. I decide who gets into witness protection. I run everything."

She shifted her feet, putting them flat on the floor.

Adam knew she understood. He had a plan to get her out of there and she was prepped to do her part.

"You're with the Justice Department," she said.

"I see you do recognize my name."

"I think it's ironic you work there since you don't seem to know what justice means."

John's nails dug into his palms. From this position, Adam could see the marks.

"I earned this job," John said.

"By killing people?"

"By being better at my job than anyone else."

Adam planned to use that ego against John. The man didn't expect an attack from underneath him. Didn't believe he could be stopped. Adam knew better.

"They know you're involved." Maddie twisted her hands several times.

Adam saw the movement but couldn't get to her fingers without giving his true condition away. He was about to turn back to John when he noticed she had one finger pointed toward the ground. He struggled to understand the message.

When she shook the finger, he got it. A countdown.

He tapped her ankle once to let her know he was watching. Then she held out two fingers and he knew the time had come to do something.

"They have the evidence against you," she added.

John stood back up again. "Not possible."

"Very possible."

The more sure she sounded, the more defensive he got. "I've had enough of this."

So had Adam. When Maddie reached three, he made his move. In a fluid motion, he lifted his arm and felt the knife slide into his palm. Curling around the chair leg and out of Maddie's kicking range, Adam clicked the weapon and stabbed the blade as hard as he could into John's ankle.

Adam sliced across tendon and heard the man scream. John doubled over, his hands grabbing for his leg. As he did, Maddie's foot connected with his jaw.

The entire action took but a few seconds. It played out slowly in Adam's mind, but from shift to throw, he didn't give John or Banner a chance to react.

And now he progressed to the next step. He slid across the floor, aiming for Banner's legs. This time Banner was ready. He jumped out of the way and lifted the gun, ready to slam the end into Adam's head.

"Enough!" John's scream tore through the cabin.

He held a gun on Maddie as he pulled the knife out of his leg with his other hand. The anguished cry turned to a furious stream of swearing. Blood spurted through his fingers. The weapon wavered in his fist.

He was a mass of fury. A man no longer on

the edge, but one who had passed over to the other side.

Panic flooded through Adam. He could handle guns and goons but crazy was something different. Seeing John's flushed red cheeks and rage-filled eyes put them in a different place. John could kill Maddie just for the joy of it and Adam wouldn't be able to get to her in time.

He knew Maddie recognized the turn, too. Her wide eyes pleaded with Adam to do something.

"Let's calm down." Adam sat up with his hand raised and his heart pounding hard enough to push right out of his chest. "We can figure this out."

"Who else knows?" John shouted the question.

Adam hoped Zach was close enough to hear the outburst and come running. From the blood covering John's hand, Adam tried to figure out if he'd hit a vital artery. If so, John only had so long before his strength would weaken. Adam had to make the minutes last to give both options a chance.

"What are we talking about here, John?"

A gun poked into the back of Adam's head. "Answer the man's question," Banner said.

Adam guessed the distance between his arm and Banner's leg, how quickly he could get Banner to the floor and how much time he could take before John launched a counterattack on Maddie. It didn't add up. He could get Banner down, but that left the insane man on the other side of the room.

As he calculated, he replied, "There's just me. I figured it out while I was in that pool. I came right here."

"That's not what she said." John tried to stand up, but his ankle wouldn't hold his weight. His shoes slipped in the blood pool, sending him falling.

Adam raised his hand to punch out Banner's knee, but the man's hand pressed down on Adam's shoulder. "I will kill her if you try."

John struggled to get up. He fell over Maddie's chair, the gun inching closer to her face.

She pulled back, putting as much distance as possible between her face and the weapon, just as the gun behind him dug deeper into his skull.

"Do not move." John's words slurred.

"You're in charge," Adam said.

He saw Maddie eye John's arm. Adam gave a small shake of his head to stop her. From that distance, he wouldn't be able to reach her in time to help her.

"That's right." John sneered. "You don't even see what's happening."

"Tell me."

"It's playing out right under your nose."

Adam's investigative instinct kicked into gear. "The person you're working with."

"She thinks you know everything." John waved the gun in front of Maddie. "But you don't have a clue how close it is."

After fighting to his knees, John rested his arm over the back of Maddie's chair and pulled himself up until he balanced his body around hers and pointed the gun at her middle.

"Easy now," Adam said, praying John would go down and stay there.

"Why should I listen to you?"

"I'm the one with the information. Not her."

"Tell me what you know or I shoot her. And you know all about stomach wounds." John pressed the muzzle against her and moved it around until he inched her shirt up and the metal touched her skin. "She'll bleed and writhe in pain, and you will watch it all from the front row."

Having violence touch the same places he once kissed blew a hole through Adam's control. He pressed down on the anger spiraling through him as he tried to stay focused. Losing his head now would only make things worse for her.

He played the odds in his head. If he dived for John, he might get to Maddie before a bullet. Banner would shoot, but Adam didn't care about dying if he could stay alive long enough to shield her.

Zach had to be close by. The guard at the door hadn't run in at John's shouting. It had to be a good sign.

Adam held on to that hope. "This isn't necessary, John."

"She'll die slow. You'll see the life pour out of her. Is that what you want?"

Right now Maddie was leaning into John. Adam tried to figure out why. She should want to pull away, not get close.

"No." His comment was for her, but he said it to John.

She got the message, because she looked up. Her eyes darted to the left then back in front again. When she did it a second time, Adam knew she did not intend to sit there and wait to be rescued or die. That wasn't her style anyway. She was taking control.

Her intense stare bored into him. "Please, Adam."

"Listen to your woman," John said.

She nodded. "You need to push back here. Bend, Adam."

Please. Push back. Bend. She was talking in code and he wasn't figuring it out.

"I can't take the risk," he said.

John tightened his hold on her. "I will kill her."

Adam blocked out John and Banner and everything else and focused on Maddie. He needed to understand. "Look at me."

She did. Then her eyes shifted to the left again. "Just do it. I can do my part, but you have to do yours."

Banner lifted his hand off Adam's shoulder. "What are they talking about?"

"Now!" Maddie screamed the order as she tipped her chair, smashing it into John and sending him crashing to the floor.

As the chair fell, Adam turned his attention to Banner. He punched the space right above his kneecap and watched it buckle. In that brief moment, Adam had the advantage. He aimed all his weight at Banner's knees. He heard a pop and a shout of pain.

Adam was rolling before Banner hit the

floor. Adam jumped on top of the bigger man, grabbing for the gun. Banner had fight left in him. He roared with fury as he tried to throw Adam off him and aim his weapon at Adam's forehead. They wrestled, shifting and moving, the gun bobbling as it inched first closer to Banner then to Adam.

Banner kicked but Adam ignored the shots. Using all of his strength, Adam pressed down, pushing the gun close to Banner's face and trying to mess up his grip. When he tried to adjust his hands, Adam grabbed the muzzle and pointed it away from his face.

Twisting the metal, Adam got the better position on the gun. With a bouncing push, he slammed his body into Banner's stomach and the end of the gun into his nose.

Blood poured down Banner's face and his hands as he held his nose. Adam hit him again in the side of his head to knock him out.

Adam jumped to his feet and turned in time to see Maddie's chair land on John and the gun spin across the floor. He stopped it with his foot. When John slapped the floor, reaching for the knife that had once poked out of his leg, Adam fired. The shot clipped John in the neck. Air gurgled and blood spurted everywhere like a scene from a horror movie.

The splash of violence and death stopped Adam for a second. He stood rooted to the floor until he heard Maddie screaming his name.

He sprang across the room and shifted the chair off John. Adam ignored the dying man and reached for the cables around Maddie's hands.

Adam tugged on the bindings just as the front door banged open. He brought up his gun, prepared to kill as many times as he had to for her.

"It's me." Zach called out the warning before he stepped in the doorway. Luke followed right after.

Both glanced at the bloodbath and went to work. Luke ripped off his outer shirt, leaving behind only his Kevlar and a T-shirt. He wadded up the dark shirt in a ball and pressed it against John's neck.

"Who are you working for?" Luke asked the question, but John's eyes were glassy and his face too filled with fear. The gunshot might have cut his vocal cords, because he could only gasp and wheeze.

Zach checked Banner's pulse as he relieved the unconscious man of his weapons. "We've got a live one. Maybe he can answer some questions."

Adam only cared about Maddie. With bloody hands, he tore at the cables until Luke threw him a knife. In two seconds he had her free and in his arms.

"I'm sorry." He rocked her as he apologized over and over.

"I was so scared." She mumbled the words into his shoulder.

"You didn't show it." He glanced over her to glare at Zach. "Nothing like cutting it close."

"Hey, man. I had to take out three. You only had two."

Adam used the chatter to calm his senses. His synapses kept firing and his body trembled with the sudden comedown. "You had Luke's help."

Zach looked around the room. "Good point, but we still got here in time."

"To see it end."

Zach nodded in Maddie's direction. "Looks like you did okay."

She stirred. Adam let his hands roam over her hair and down her back, as if confirming that she was alive.

He lifted her head and cupped her cheeks in his palms. "You're okay now."

Despite the chaos around them, he kissed her. He poured all his need and desire into it. His lips traveled over hers, trying to wipe away the bruises and pain.

She broke away, her lips swollen and her tone breathless and serious. "Take me home."

They were in her home. This disaster zone belonged to her and he couldn't leave her here. She wasn't safe and he refused to let her go.

"Where is that exactly?"

"To the Recovery warehouse."

Chapter Eighteen

Maddie brushed her foot against Adam's bare leg. After the initial rush of questions and Caleb's insistence that they both have a medical check, the crowd of Recovery well-wishers had finally cleared out of the warehouse. Two hours of lovemaking later, she sprawled at Adam's side on the big bed at the top of the stairs.

They'd skipped lunch…and then dinner. The sun vanished as night fell. Still, they didn't leave the bed. After the awful few days that came before, she loved the feel of soft sheets against her skin.

She loved Adam even more. She dared to hope her streak of bad men and worse luck had ended. With Adam she saw a future. Being in the program for years, she hadn't ever let herself make plans. She'd lived every day for the day in front of her only. Survive, sleep and start it all again. That had been her mantra.

She'd crossed off the days on her calendar on a countdown to the time when Knevin found her. Her whole life was focused on that point. All about drills and maneuvers.

She didn't want to run any longer. She craved normalcy.

She'd looked at Claire and Mia and Avery earlier and envied their calm reassurance that they would be fine in the face of danger because the Recovery team would make it so. They fought beside the men they loved, met them on equal terms and did not back down at danger.

Maddie had heard the stories, so she knew. She also guessed that no one ever told her new female friends where to live and how to act.

She could have all that but only outside the program. The risks were great, but if Knevin wanted to send waves of soldiers after her, she'd find a way to deal with it. What the past few days taught her was that life inside WitSec was not any safer for her than a life on the outside.

Adam stopped yawning and stared at her. "You seem to be concentrating really hard on something."

"Just thinking."

"Sounds like the same thing."

"I guess." Her hand rested on his chest and his warm skin pressed against her everywhere their bodies touched. The sheets draped low on his waist, leaving some of his most impressive parts free to her touch and view.

A pillow tucked under her back helped ease the spasms that shook her on the ride back from West Virginia. By the time they stepped in the door, Adam was apoplectic and screaming for Caleb's help.

That all happened hours ago, before the showers of concern. Now she was comfortable and happy. The back pain and small aches couldn't break through her good mood.

Adam reached over to the nightstand and picked up a bottle. He shook it, rattling the pills inside. "You should take your meds now."

"I will when you do."

"Caleb is going to yell."

"Then he can yell at both of us."

Adam acted as if she was the only one who came back home broken and exhausted. He conveniently forgot how he took the brunt of the beatings. He'd been cut and hit, shot and nearly drowned. One would think he'd done nothing more than enjoyed a leisurely drive into the country. It was so bad that Claire actually took his clothes and promised to throw them away.

Maddie appreciated every cut and bruise on his body and had spent a long time kissing each one. She could still remember how she'd screamed with pleasure when he returned the favor.

He dropped the bottle and wrapped his arms around her. One cradled her head. The other swept across her body to pull her close. "I want to stay awake and ready in case you need me."

"For what?"

He wiggled his eyebrows. "Anything."

"I'm thinking we need to rest before we 'anything' again."

He laughed as he nuzzled his nose against her neck. "Tell me the truth about something."

She pressed her head deeper in the pillow to give him access. "Again I say, I will if you will."

"Uh, okay."

Her heart did a jumping twirl. "Really?"

His head popped up. "Wait, what?"

"You want me to talk. Well, I will if you answer a few questions of mine. You're not the only one with a wild case of curiosity."

"I was talking about your back."

"Oh."

"With everything that's happened, all the falls and shocks, I wanted to make sure it was okay." He leaned up on an elbow and stared down at her. "What were you talking about?"

She bit down on her lip, debating whether to take the next step or retreat. "I'm trying to even the field."

"Maybe I'm slow from all the sex—"

"Or the hit on the head with a gun."

"That, too. But, what are you getting at?"

She trailed a finger over his chest and down to his flat stomach. "We've been all over each other, fought through unbelievable circumstances, and I still don't know anything about you."

"That's not true."

He didn't physically move away, but she suddenly felt a chill blow between them. His hand stopped caressing the sensitive area under her breast.

His reaction tempted her to pull back and talk about this later. But one look into his confused eyes and she pushed aside more thoughts of running, even emotionally. He didn't understand.

If she could get through to him... She had to.

"Is your middle name Stuart? I don't know something as mundane as that."

He blinked at her. "Michael."

"What?"

"Adam Michael Wright."

She pressed up on her elbows and sighed when he moved back, putting space between them. He sat with his back against the headboard and his hands on his lap. All the heat from their lovemaking evaporated. He could not have looked less receptive or willing to talk.

She feared he didn't want to understand. "Come on, Adam. You know what I mean."

"Not really."

"We're talking about the intimate details of our lives."

"Why?"

"Isn't it obvious?"

"Because we're in bed? But none of that other stuff matters or even belongs in here with us."

His words slapped at her. "How can you say that?"

"Your life was made up and handed to you and I don't care." He spoke as if she meant something to him but the closed-for-business sign was clear on his face.

The truth shouted through her brain. It was the one bat he held and he verbally hit her with it. "This is about the drugs, isn't it?"

He ran his hand through his hair and exhaled loud enough to shake the walls. "I don't care about your past. I've said it. I can write it. I'll even take a blood oath if you want."

For the first time since she met him she knew he was lying. He obsessed about the drug charges. Maybe he pushed the idea out of his head long enough to take her to bed, but it came rushing back as soon as they started talking. He saw her as a woman who would give drugs to kids, and that made her sick.

"No, you do care. That's the point, Adam. You've just decided to be the big man and forgive me for the drugs."

He threw up his hands. "Is that a bad thing?"

Her heartbeat stumbled. It was as if the words reached in and squeezed hard enough to cause damage.

"Maddie, look—"

When he reached out to her, she scrambled to the far side of the bed and stood up. She grabbed the blanket from the floor and wrapped it around her. The idea of standing there naked was more than she could take.

"Were you a hacker?" she asked him.

"What?"

"You heard me."

"That's not—"

She folded the blanket in a wad and held it between her breasts. "Trevor Walters knows more about you than I do."

"Where is all of this coming from? You sure seemed fine with me a half hour ago."

Those remaining pieces of her heart shattered. "That's not fair."

"Right." He bounced his head against the headboard a few times. "Okay, sorry. Just explain this to me."

"When a woman wakes up and realizes she's in love, she wants to know everything about that man."

The harsh lines of his face softened. He moved to her side of the bed. "Maddie—"

"Don't." She held out her hand to keep him from coming closer. If he touched her, she'd break. She didn't have a single defense against him. "I don't want pity. I deserve more than that."

"I was going to tell you I feel the same way."

Happiness warred with despair inside her. He was handing her everything she thought she wanted, but it felt so hollow. "And?"

"That's your response?" He stood up, ignoring his nudity and raising his voice with each word. "I tell you how I feel and you just stare at me."

"You didn't even say the words. You basically said ditto. You don't take any risk or put yourself out there." Her shoulders slumped, but she held her head high. "Don't you understand? I've lived my life in this false fog for years. I've had to lie about who I am and push people away. Now I want something more. With you."

"I want that, too."

"But you still won't let me in."

"You're here with me. You are the only person I've ever told about Recovery."

It was something. But not enough. "That's a job, not you."

He rubbed his face. When his hands dropped, she saw the storm in his eyes. He wasn't going to back down.

"I don't know what you want from me." His voice was soft and scary deep.

"Everything."

"Put it in guy terms. Just say the words."

"I did."

"I'm not a mind reader."

It was so easy and he was making it so hard. She wanted to reach out but she couldn't do it alone. "I want your love and your trust. I want to know who you are and what you want."

"Don't you think that's a little much? We've only known each other a week."

She lost her breath. The words stabbed through her so hard and so fast, she looked down expecting to see blood on the floor. "You're right."

"Let's back up here. I'm just saying we need time. Don't read more into it."

It hurt to talk. To look at him. To stand there and not fall in a heap to the floor. "If I honestly thought you would tear down that wall and let me in, I'd give you all the time you needed. I'd wait and hope and love you."

"Then do that."

"But that's not who you are."

His lips fell flat. "How do you know?"

He kept swinging. He was not going to back down until he destroyed her.

"My past disgusts you, or what you think it is does. I get that. Instead of dealing with it, you've decided to pick up from right now and never look back."

"I don't see why that's a bad thing."

Every bit of hope and light shriveled inside her. "And that's the problem."

She dropped the blanket, no longer caring

about being naked. She'd been stripped bare already. She picked up the shirt Mia had given her and pulled it over her head. While she looked for her underwear, she felt Adam's hand on her arm.

He spun her around. "So, you're leaving? That's it?"

"Yes."

"I don't say what you want, so you get mad at me and run?" He snorted. "Of course. Why should I be surprised? Your whole life is about running and hiding."

She lifted her chin. "Not anymore."

Chapter Nineteen

The call for a meeting came the next morning. Newly minted congressman David Brennan insisted Luke come in for an afternoon meeting. Adam needed to get out of the warehouse and catch some air without the temptation of Maddie, so he volunteered to go along. It wasn't until he was in the car that Luke told him David wanted to see them both.

The request didn't make any more sense an hour later when he sat with Luke and watched David ease into his impressive blue leather chair. The Capitol could be seen out the window behind him. It was a perfect scene for a man in power.

Adam knew David came by his the honest way. He'd worked up from the lowly positions in the office to win the special election for Bram Walters's congressional seat when he died.

"I have a job for you," David said.

Adam didn't want to state the obvious, but he wanted to be done. Even though he volunteered to come along, every minute away from Maddie made him nervous.

He needed space, but this was too much. Her current mood left him speechless. He knew after a few days of calm she'd settle down and they could have a decent conversation, but until then he'd worry she'd do something rash.

He went for the hard truth. "You're a congressman."

David glanced at the flag next to his window. "I am aware of that."

"You want to employ Recovery?" Luke asked.

"A man I believed in and worked for got involved in a scheme that led to the murder of innocent women. Career civil servants acted in such deplorable ways as to threaten the viability of the protection program." David stopped and took a breath. "And now I sit here with a stack of files and wonder if it is over."

"We don't think so," Luke said.

"Why?"

Adam decided to speak plain. "It's too clean."

David smiled. "And that's a bad thing?"

"Generally." Adam could give a list to support his position but left it at that.

David reached down and pulled out a thick file folder. "I have a deal to make with you."

Luke shot Adam a you've-got-to-be-kidding-me look. "The last deal I made I regretted."

David continued. "I can't speak to whatever that was, but I can tell you mine."

"Go ahead," Adam said, suddenly curious.

"I will hand over all the documents Bram left behind." David tapped his hand against the top of the file he held. "I can get you access to John Tate's personal finances and private correspondence, including his computer, so you can attempt to trace the money trail."

This part of the offer was too good to be true. Adam's skepticism battled with his excitement. "How are you managing that one?"

"Mrs. Tate, like Trevor before her, wants to preserve a memory of her loved one for others. She has children. She doesn't want her husband's name tainted."

Adam had reached his limit on reputation saving. "People are dead. The public deserves to know why."

"The public needs to believe that WitSec

works. Without that, the judicial system will falter," David said in true politician style.

Luke shook his head. "I'm not convinced."

David handed the file to Luke. "I will get you all the documents you need. You can confirm if this rampage is over and if the other participants are safe. We can end this."

"And in return?"

David pressed his lips together as if he was trying to find the right words to promote his idea. "The findings stay between us."

Anger welled in Adam's throat. "That feels like a cover-up to me."

"Think of it as a celebration of the greater good." David stared at Luke. "I'm sure you want to ensure the safety of your wife. Congratulations on the pregnancy, by the way."

Adam tapped his fingers against the arm of the chair. The frustration pinging around inside him had nowhere to go. "I have to say you've taken to this politician thing quickly."

"My only point is that some of you now have something worth losing." This time David looked at Adam. "Speaking of which, I will personally guarantee Ms. Timmons's safety."

Adam stopped moving. "Excuse me?"

"Until we know how deep this goes and if

the corruption still rages in WitSec, I have come up with alternate arrangements for her through the Secret Service."

Adam turned the idea over in his mind and whichever way he looked at it, he hated it. No way was he letting her out of his sight. "She can stay with us."

"She needs to go back into the program eventually. I have connections and can—"

"No." She wasn't going anywhere. Adam vowed to protect her.

"She'll have a new identity and a chance at a life without gunmen following her."

"She's safer with us."

"Is she?" David rushed on before they could answer. "Well, you look over what I have in the file and let me know about the deal."

Luke finally spoke up. "We'll talk it over. The whole team has to agree, and I can't guarantee that."

"I appreciate that." David handed Luke a card. "And I will call you about Ms. Timmons tomorrow."

Adam waited for Luke to say something. When he didn't, Adam stood up. "She'll leave when it's clear she is not in danger."

"She's still a potential loose end. She's the only one still alive from this WitSec cash-for-information scheme that we know of. Money has been paid."

Adam was tired of the lecture. "I know the score."

David took the dressing-down without getting upset. "Then you know this Knevin person was not the only individual she testified against. She took down the entire drug operation."

Luke nodded. "And that could make some folks very angry."

Adam felt the conversation spinning out of control. "I don't think—"

David cut him off. "Which is why I'll personally get her tomorrow."

ADAM WALKED FAST, but Luke caught up. He matched strides as they neared the elevator. Before Adam could hit the button, Luke stepped in front of him.

"Are you really going to let her go?" Luke asked.

Adam couldn't take this. Not now. He'd fought with Maddie and spent a silent breakfast ignoring her chatter when Zach showed up with doughnuts.

Now Luke. He was one of the people Adam

respected most in the world. Their bond ran deep and Adam feared losing it.

"She's not Claire."

"I'm not sure what that means, but you're right. Maddie is her own person, with baggage and an attitude and a threat on her life that would destroy most people."

Adam didn't need a list of her virtues or her troubles. He loved her. He didn't understand her worth a damn and was sick with thinking she wouldn't be there when he got back, but he loved her. He made Zach promise to watch her, but that was no guarantee.

Adam glared at Luke. "Your point?"

"She's not easy."

No kidding. She'd nearly killed him when she put on her clothes and fumbled her way down the steps to get away from him. She proved she'd rather handle the pain than talk to him.

Adam noticed Luke kept staring at him. "I'm still not following you."

"She's complicated, but…"

"What?" Adam snapped.

"I've never seen another woman who could handle you. Who walked by and had you panting."

Adam turned around and leaned his back against the wall. "That's not the basis for a relationship."

"I'm impressed you can say that word."

Adam closed his eyes, but when he opened them again none of his problems had disappeared. "You're not funny."

"You ever wonder why you find her so attractive?" Luke laughed. "And don't give me that look. My investigative skills are pretty good and you haven't been subtle about your feelings. I was in that room when you untied her. I saw both of you and that wasn't just respect happening there."

"She's beautiful."

Luke frowned. "That's it? It's that simple for you? She looks good?"

"Yes." Adam's stomach rolled on the lie.

Luke's eyes narrowed. He looked like a prosecutor moving in for the kill on a witness. "So, you don't care if she leaves."

"That's different. She's not ready."

Luke hit the elevator button. "Honestly, man. You're the one who's not ready."

"Meaning?"

"She's way ahead of you and I'm hoping like hell you catch up before it's too late."

MADDIE DIDN'T NEED a suitcase because she didn't own a single material possession. No clothes. No house. Every item that held a memory had been taken long ago. She'd burned her photographs. The items she'd collected since being renamed Maddie were back in West Virginia and she'd never be going there again.

She'd probably end up in Kentucky or somewhere out west. Her first name would likely still start with an *M* because that was the protocol. She had secretarial skills and could cook. She hoped they could find her a job doing one of those.

She dropped to the bed with Adam's shirt in her hands. Lifting it to her face, she inhaled his distinct scent. She was wrong. She had something to take with her: a broken heart and an abandoned shirt.

"What are you doing?" Adam's deep voice was as sensual as a caress.

It had the power to crush her common sense and change all her plans. He had no idea how much he meant to her or how easy it would be for him if he just opened his heart to her.

She stood up and wadded the shirt in a ball behind her back. "Packing."

"I guess my question is why." He walked

over and didn't stop until he stood right in front of her.

His hand slipped behind her back and gently pulled her arm forward. He stared down at his blue shirt.

She shoved it at his chest and walked over to the small bureau across from the end of the bed. Nothing in the drawers belonged to her, but she needed space. She busied her hands with the comb and brush sitting on top.

Avery had bought them for her. Maddie realized that every time she had a need, someone close to Adam filled it. She looked up into his green eyes.

Except for one.

"It's time for me to go." Her voice cracked, but she forced the sentence out.

He shook his head. "It's not safe."

Leave it to him to think about the logistics and rescue aspects. "Oh, Adam. I haven't been safe for a long time."

"What if I told you I didn't want you to go?"

Her insides whirled. She tamped down the hope sparked by his words. "I'd ask you why."

"That's not very romantic."

He was killing her by inches. Just when she erected a wall against him, he broke through and opened another breach.

Rather than let hope build, she sought to squash it. "I'm waiting for the look of panic to come over you."

"What are you talking about?"

"You have it now." She leaned back against the dresser and pointed at his handsome face.

"I've had a hard time figuring out why a woman without a past would care about mine." He closed in on her until he pinned her against the dresser and he stood between her legs.

"I don't care about school mascots and first kisses," she said. "That's not what I'm talking about, but I give up trying to explain it."

"Good, because none of that has anything to do with who I am now or what I want from life." She sighed, trying to ease the tightness in her chest. "I'm serious."

"I was good at two things as a kid. They were skills as far apart as you can imagine. Football and computers. One kept me inside and the other took me out."

She was almost afraid to say anything. She didn't want him to stop talking. But he just stood there, so close and so tempting, with a smile on his face. "I bet only one of those made you popular."

He winked. "I did okay."

She loved this side of him. The joking and

fun side. It was bittersweet to experience it now when the end was in sight.

"I went to college on a football scholarship but spent most of my time on computers and chasing girls. Not two things that usually go together, I know. But having the jersey helped with the latter."

Imagining a younger version of him made her smile.

"And lucky for me, my school didn't care much about my grades or class attendance so long as I made tackles, so I could practice my hacking skills and skip science classes."

He straightened up and rubbed his hands up and down her arms. The gentle touch set off fireworks in her stomach. She dared to hope his willingness to share his past meant something, but she dreaded being wrong again.

"I honed my computer skills but not as much as I thought. Senior year I got nabbed by the FBI."

If he did cartwheels down the stairs she would have been less stunned. "What?"

"You know what the Defense Mapping Agency is?"

"No."

"Well, the folks in charge there don't like it when you get into their computer security system and change their passwords." His fingers massaged the back of her neck.

The touch soothed her battered nerves. "You were arrested?"

"Almost, but I ended up with a job offer, a steady income and the ability to pay rent instead. Part of some program where the FBI enlisted hackers, tried to make us good citizens while they used our skills."

Every piece formed a picture of who he was and why. Knowing this meant everything to her.

But she needed to know that sharing it all meant something to him. "Why are you talking now?"

He kissed her then, soft and short. His lips pressed against hers then left before she could pull him in deeper. "Because, Margaret, we all have a past."

If she hadn't loved him already she would have fallen forever in love with him right then. "You remembered."

"Of course."

"I wish you could, but you can't call me that," she whispered against his mouth.

"I prefer Maddie anyway. The point is that I understand there's more to you than a simple name. You are complex and fierce."

Tears rushed to the back of her eyes.

"Will you let me know more? Let me know all of you?" She really wanted a future, but the road there ran through the past.

When he brushed his thumb over her lips instead of answering, she held her breath. The halfway point was right in front of him. She just needed him to take the mental step.

"After my fiancée died in a car crash caused by a drunk driver, I left the desk job for one that carried a gun. I wanted to fight and save and put away anyone who broke the law."

Maddie felt only sadness about his incredible loss. It explained so much about the walls he erected. "I'm sorry."

"It was years ago."

"But it's part of who you are and what shapes you." Part of what she loved most, that capacity to give comfort and excitement at the same time.

She'd been so convinced he didn't feel, that very little touched him. Knowing he'd lost a fiancée made her see she'd been wrong. He felt and lost and feared his life playing out that way again.

She understood. She didn't bury a love. She lost herself. It was a different kind of trauma.

"Rod gave me a chance when he handed me

a weapon. I don't know what's happening with him now or where he went, but I'll always be thankful that he made that note in his file that brought me to you."

"Adam." She put her hands on his face and repeated the words that had killed everything before. "I never dealt drugs."

He turned one of her hands and kissed her palm. "I know."

His words, so clear and strong, rang through her. "I… Since when? You didn't trust me before."

He did now. He shook with the intensity of it and made her believe.

"Some part of me always knew." He licked a sensual path around her palm. "The rest of me denied."

"Why?"

"If you were everything you appeared to be—smart and beautiful and honest and strong—then I wouldn't have any defense against you. I fought it until it became ridiculous and even Zach and Luke thought I'd lost my mind."

"I would never do that to—"

"You don't have to say it again or doubt my belief in you. I know."

She hadn't cried in years before meeting

Adam. Her emotions ran out of control around him. Even now, she fought back tears.

"For a guy who professes to stink at intimacy, you're doing a good job."

"Well, hold on, because you're about to see my bossy side."

She sniffled. "I can take it."

"You are not going anywhere tomorrow. This whole plan about Luke meeting with David Brennan and him handing you off to the Secret Service? Never going to happen." The sweetness left his voice. He was ordering her now and not leaving any room for doubt.

But she loved that he was fighting for her.

Their main problem still remained and he had to be honest about it. It was one thing for her to agree to take the risk. She couldn't make that decision for him. "Being near me isn't safe."

"You're kidding with that, right? Do you understand what I do for a living? How much death I see?"

"I'm in the program."

"You were. Now you're in *my* program. The guys who were supposed to protect you failed, so it's my turn."

"I can't argue with that."

His dimple appeared and the smile came

right after. "And then there's the part where I love you."

There it was. The final piece. Joy filled her, wiping out all the sadness and pain that had come before. "You finally said it."

"I've been feeling it since ten minutes after I met you."

She snorted. "I don't believe that."

"Your pies were really good at that diner."

She burst out laughing. "Funny guy."

"I can't promise it will be smooth or that I'll stop being a jerk, but I can promise to love and protect you."

She wound her arms around his neck and brought his mouth down to hers. The kiss soothed and electrified, calmed and lit a fire. It went on until she lost her breath and her inhibitions fell away.

When she finally lifted her head she believed in the promise of tomorrow for the first time since she was fourteen. "And I'll love and protect you right back."

He wiggled his eyebrows at her. "I think we should start now."

She peeked over his shoulder. "Is everyone still downstairs?"

"Claire pushed them all out when I came up here. Luke said something about me needing to get my head out of my—"

Maddie touched a finger to Adam's lips as happiness overwhelmed her. "I get it."

"Getting the details sorted out might take some time, but I do love you and we will figure it out."

She'd run for so long that she was mentally exhausted, but with him she could be herself. She could share her fears and fight her demons. He would never hurt her or leave her. He'd made a vow and he would keep it.

A woman couldn't ask for more.

"You know what I think?" She cuddled in even closer.

"You can say just about anything right now and I'll agree."

"Smart man."

"I'm slow, but I have staying power." He wrapped his arms around her and started walking backward to the bed.

"Is that your personal motto?"

"Maybe."

She liked it. It fit him. "You know what mine is?"

"Tell me."

"With you I can do anything."

"I'm willing to try a little 'anything' right now."

She threw her head back and laughed. Then his mouth covered hers and she didn't think at all.

Chapter Twenty

Trevor sat at his desk and downed his third glass of scotch. The windows behind his desk provided a wide-open view of the city. The lights usually calmed him. Tonight nothing removed the sting.

He'd gotten everything he wanted. Russell and John were gone. The Recovery Team would stay out of his business. If anyone had the tape, the person wasn't talking.

But the price had been high. He'd made a deal with Luke that would keep his company running and his public reputation sound, but the worry would always be there.

Trevor knew he had lost his advantage. He would no longer be able to play the game the same way. His edge had been dulled.

And it was not over.

He knew John's partner would come calling. Maybe not to ask for help, but there would be a price. Luke suspected Trevor's involvement. Someone out there had proof of it. Money and resources. Sure, Trevor kept his men and Orion's name out of any trial, but that would not matter.

John's partner was willing to kill. He knew when to retreat and how to hide his identity. He was on the inside and until recently above suspicion. He seemed to have an endless supply of gunmen, and money to fund them. And if he had any fear he was not showing it.

The person—Rod or Trevor or some possible third party who had not shown his hand yet—was tying up loose ends. Trevor had never been a loose end. Until now.

The phone on the edge of his desk rang. It was the after-hours line that only a few people knew. It could be his ex or his son or even Sela. Could be but wasn't.

This was the call. The one he had sat all night waiting to receive.

Trevor picked up on the fourth ring.

LUKE THREW DOWN his pen and folded his arms behind his neck. He sat at the head of the table and took the lead as if he was born to the role.

Adam's confidence in his friend never wavered. They'd talked out the scene in Trevor's office and Adam knew he'd never hear about it again. The group was forgiving and their loyalty ran that deep.

"So, we're agreed." Luke rocked back in his chair as he glanced around the conference table at Zach and Adam then up at the flat-screen television where Caleb and Holden were dialed in for the conference. Maddie leaned against the sink sipping tea, but Luke looked for a head nod from her, too.

Zach spoke for all of them. "We're in."

Luke put his hand on the stack of files to his right. "We take David's deal and follow this through to the end. We keep going no matter what we find."

"Even if that means the line ends with Vince." Adam forced himself to say the rest. "Or Rod."

"What about Trevor?" Caleb asked.

Luke's neutral expression gave way to a tense jaw. "We have a deal with him. We'll abide by it."

"I'm sorry. I know you did that for me." Maddie mumbled the apology over the top of her mug.

Luke's response came swift and sure. "Don't be."

"If we'd have time for a vote we all would

have agreed that your safety was more important than taking Trevor down." Zach said the words, but they spoke up in agreement.

She glanced at Adam. "Thank you."

"And between us and the feds, we'll get Knevin. In the meantime, nothing will happen to you here."

"Sounds good to me."

He watched her standing there and realized he loved her more each minute. "You're one of us now."

Holden laughed. "That's a good thing, right?"

Luke cleared his throat to get them back on track. "Surveillance on Trevor, his assistant and Vince begins tomorrow. Adam will get the communications set up and guard Maddie. Caleb and Mia will work on the forensics we gathered from Maddie's house. Zach will take Orion. We'll finish this thing."

Adam reached over and grabbed a folder from Luke's pile. "We may as well start now."

"I'm ready," Maddie said.

He knew that was true. She was ready to move and get on with life. So was he, but he had to free her from the ghosts that haunted her so they could have a future.

And that future would start right now.

* * * * *

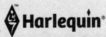